PRAISE FOR *DARK*

'Tony Birch's short stories are precious gems. Written in a deceptively simple prose, the pages of *Dark as Last Night* capture the humanity, courage and humour of characters in the midst of life.'

—The Guardian

'*Dark as Last Night* is a reminder of the lives that can be shared through the short story, and what a punch they pack when written well. In this stunning, timely collection Birch brings a softness to real and fictional spaces that is sorely needed right now.'

—Readings

'Birch's clear eye for detail, as well as for darkness and quirk of character, shines through at every turn.'

—Books+Publishing

'There are so many things to take away from *Dark as Last Night* ... Birch's skill in bringing a place and its people to life is second to none. These vignettes shine a light on the ordinary, highlighting the brief moments which define us.'

—AU Review

'This collection sings with poetic brevity. Birch writes with enthralling crisp prose, each short story dancing in the mind akin to a flashback.'

−Kill Your Darlings

'They are stories that stay with us: powerful evocations of how the past bears down on the present.'

−Australian Book Review

'Birch's version of realism gives voice to those who don't have much and shows beauty where an outside observer might find it lacking.'

−ArtsHub

Tony Birch is the author of three novels: *The White Girl*, winner of the 2020 NSW Premier's Award for Indigenous Writing, and shortlisted for the 2020 Miles Franklin Literary Award; *Ghost River*, winner of the 2016 Victorian Premier's Literary Award for Indigenous Writing; and *Blood*, which was shortlisted for the Miles Franklin Literary Award in 2012. He is also the author of *Shadowboxing* and four short story collections: *Father's Day*, *The Promise*, *Common People* and *Dark as Last Night*. He has published two poetry collections: *Broken Teeth* and *Whisper Songs*, which was shortlisted for the 2022 Margaret and Colin Roderick Literary Award. In 2017 he was awarded the Patrick White Literary Award. Tony Birch is also an activist, historian and essayist.

www.tony-birch.com

Also by Tony Birch

DARK AS
LAST NIGHT

TONY BIRCH

First published 2021 by University of Queensland Press
PO Box 6042, St Lucia, Queensland 4067 Australia
Reprinted 2021

This edition published 2023

University of Queensland Press (UQP) acknowledges the Traditional Owners
and their custodianship of the lands on which UQP operates. We pay our respects
to their Ancestors and their descendants, who continue cultural and spiritual
connections to Country. We recognise their valuable contributions to Australian
and global society.

uqp.com.au
reception@uqp.com.au

Cover design by Jenna Lee
Adapted by Post Pre-press Group, Brisbane
Author photo by Savanna Kruger
Typeset in Bembo by Post Pre-press Group, Brisbane
Printed in Australia by McPherson's Printing Group

University of Queensland Press is assisted
by the Australian Government through
the Australia Council, its arts funding and
advisory body.

A catalogue record for this book is available from the National Library of Australia.

ISBN 978 0 7022 6633 1 (pbk)
ISBN 978 0 7022 6489 4 (epdf)
ISBN 978 0 7022 6490 0 (epub)
ISBN 978 0 7022 6491 7 (kindle)

University of Queensland Press uses papers that are natural, renewable and
recyclable products made from wood grown in well-managed forests and other
controlled sources. The logging and manufacturing processes conform to the
environmental regulations of the country of origin.

For Charlie Atticus Burke
– arrived in the world on 27 November 2020 –
a cousin for Isabel Kit and Archie James.

CONTENTS

DARK AS LAST NIGHT

IN THE FINAL WEEKS BEFORE my younger brother was due to be born, my mother carried her weighty stomach around the house, cooking and scrubbing in silence. Her legs were laced with dark varicose veins and her face worn to the bone. Her body would shake when she heard Dad's workboots scrape against the front doorstep, announcing his arrival home. When he was sober my father would inspect the house forensically, like a social worker expecting a slip-up – running a finger across the kitchen tabletop checking for grime, opening drawers and cupboards, working his fingers like an abacus to count the small change left over from shopping. Finally, he'd check his watch to be certain his dinner had been delivered to the table on time. Six o'clock sharp.

Drunkenness played tricks with my father's body and mind. There was no scraping of boots or inventories on beer nights. He'd stagger down the street from the tram stop, his military stride deserting him. The clinking of bottles in a brown paper bag tucked under an arm and a deranged smile was a sure sign of a night of mayhem ahead.

My father's rage taught me to become invisible from a young age. At kick-off I'd retreat to hiding places secreted throughout the house – under the old pedal sewing machine in the hallway or behind the couch in the front room were favoured spots, until he hunted me down and I had to abandon them. Sometimes I'd sneak to the back corner of our muddy yard and perch on the splintered wooden toilet seat, listening to rats scurry across the floor.

My mother coped best when his explosions erupted and ended quickly, rather than his slow-burn routine of domestic control. On the nights fuelled by alcohol, dinner was often the first casualty. He'd stand up from the table as if he was about to make a civic speech and shout an obscenity about the undercooked vegetables or overcooked meat. The kitchen chair would crash to the floor and the dinner plate would smash against a wall. The following morning I'd sit at the table eating breakfast in silence, occasionally glancing up at a lump of mashed potato, squashed peas or a smear of gravy stuck to the wall. I learned early in life not to point and ask, 'What's that?'

Some nights he preferred outdoor sport. He'd open the back door and hurl his plate of food over the fence into the laneway behind the house, leaving the dinner scraps to stray cats. Many years later, as an adult, I became an expert at disguising the truth of my violent childhood. I held court with stories about my *crazy dad*, the demented Olympian who practised the discus and shot-put with a full roast dinner. The tales got a laugh, even from those who'd heard them many times and suspected the darker truth.

A story I never told was the one about the night the dinner plate hit the wall, shattered, and a broken shard struck my mother in the face. The *accident* was my mother's own fault, my father explained to her, as she dabbed a towel to her cheek.

'You're useless,' he said, as if that was enough to explain what had happened.

Mum was not a woman to answer back, not to my father at least. But she did that night, to my surprise. She put a hand to her cheek, looked down at her fingertips and flicked the blood onto the lino floor. 'You mean I should have ducked?' she asked. 'Is that your idea of an accident?'

'What did you say?' he roared, shocked by her insolence.

'I'm asking you if I should have ducked,' she said. 'You coward.'

Sitting at the table, afraid to move, I silently begged her not to provoke him further. *He's right*, I thought. This had to be her fault because she just couldn't keep her mouth shut. He stood up and grabbed her by the throat with one hand. He slapped her face with the other hand and shook her body ferociously. Mum wrapped her arms protectively around her stomach and turned away to shield her unborn baby. All I knew to do was run and hide, some place where he would not find me.

I pushed the back door open and ran along the side path to the front of the house. It was raining and the street was pitch black. I stopped, shaking with fear, realising I had nowhere to go.

A husky voice called out to me from the verandah next door. I saw the glow of a cigarette and the shadow of our neighbour. Little Red was a mysterious figure who kept mostly to herself and rarely spoke to anyone on the street. In the absence of truth, lurid stories had circulated about her. Some said she'd worked as a fortune-teller in Sideshow Alley with the circus or that she'd been a stripper in nightclubs. Others claimed she was a witch who cast spells on those who wronged her. People even said that she'd killed every stray cat in the street in an act of sacrifice. Another rumour, possibly the most unbelievable of all, was that she had an indoor toilet in her house. A toilet with its own room.

Little Red was a short woman, and pencil thin. She'd come by her name because of the combination of her lack of height and the flaming colour of her hair, which she wore out. 'Why doesn't that woman use hair rollers?' my mother complained, whenever we saw her in the street. The nearest word to a compliment about Little Red was that she was *exotic*, while some of the local men, including my father, said that she was nothing but a *harlot*. I didn't fully understand the meaning of the word when I was a kid, although I did know better than to repeat it.

'Come out of the rain,' Little Red called to me, her voice rasping with cigarette smoke and alcohol. 'You'll die of pneumonia standing out there, kid. Look at you. Your dress is already drenched through. Come over here, out of the weather.'

I hesitated.

'Please yourself,' she added. 'You can stay there and die of fever if you want to.'

The wind cut through my thin dress. Shivering, I shuffled forward and stepped up onto her verandah where it was dry. She took a drag on her cigarette and looked me up and down.

I'd never been this close to Little Red. In the glow of the cigarette I noticed her eyes sparkled.

'He's whacking her again, isn't he?' she said, surprising me with her directness. I dropped my head. She reached out and lifted the tip of my jaw with a manicured fingertip. 'He thumps you, too?' She frowned. Her voice was more caring than I'd imagined it to be, although it sounded *foreign*.

I sniffed the air. Little Red carried a heavy scent. It caused my nose to itch.

'How old are you, kid?' she asked.

'Nine,' I managed. 'I'll be ten at Christmas.'

'You're Rosie, aren't you? I hear your mother calling you home from the street sometimes.'

'It's Rose,' I said. 'My name is Rose.'

'Not for me. I like Rosie. We will keep it that way between us, from now on.'

From now on?

She offered me her cigarette. 'You want a smoke?'

I'd seen newsboys my age smoking cigarettes, but never a girl. 'No, thank you.'

'Cigarettes calm you down. I bet you don't know that? And that it's best if you start smoking young. My older brother, Max, he taught me to smoke when I was six. He told me it would make my lungs stronger and he was right about that. Poor Max gave up the cigarettes on the doctor's advice and now he's dead.' She chuckled. 'You're sure you won't have one?' She took a cigarette out of the packet. 'See, they have a filter.'

'No, thank you.'

'Manners,' she said, then sighed. 'You are wasted around

5

here, Rosie. You know that this neighbourhood is run by pigs?'

I'd never been asked such a question, but as soon as she said the word *pigs*, it made sense to me. My father certainly was a pig.

'How old do you think I am?' she asked. I had no idea, except she looked many years older than my mother. 'I know what you're thinking already,' she said. 'You don't want to say it, I know. I'm ancient.' She lit another cigarette, looked me in the eyes and blew out the match. 'That house must be terror for you. And your mother, she has another baby coming. What does that madman do in there to her?'

I listened to the rain beating on the iron roof above our heads. Leaking water dripped onto my shoulders and down the back of my dress.

'I understand how it is,' she said, shaking her head. 'You people. You're all the same. All you know to do is to keep your mouths shut and say nothing. The men here, they teach silence to young girls so early. I once saw many people killed because others said nothing.' She flicked her cigarette into the street and followed it with a spit of disgust. 'People say nothing and others die. It is this simple.'

She appeared to be talking to herself as much as to me and I became a little afraid of her.

'I have to go,' I said, although I couldn't think of where to go except home, which I was also afraid to do. I heard a scream from our kitchen window.

Little Red gripped my arm. 'That's your mother. You must go down to the police station and tell one of them lazy boys to come back here with you.' She pushed me from the verandah. 'You must go now.'

I'd never been inside a police station and knew better than to go near the police, men as dangerous as my father. I heard a second scream, a chilling cry.

'Go! Now!' Little Red shouted.

Without thinking about what I was doing I tucked my floral dress up into the legs of my underpants and ran down the hill to the end of the street. I passed the furniture factory that would burn to the ground the following year and sprinted past the corner shop. I dodged potholes and puddles, a truck turning into the next street, and a dog barking. I didn't stop running until I reached the steps of the police station, my lungs on fire.

I rested my hands on my hips and took some deep breaths, then freed my dress, recited two Hail Marys and walked up the stairs. I leaned my body against the wooden door, forcing it open and stood before a high wooden bench, unable to see over it. I coughed to get someone's attention. A policeman on the other side leaned over and looked down, surprised at his find. He had blue eyes and ginger hair.

'Look at yourself, girl. Have you been swimming? It's a terror of a night out there.'

I stared up at him. His head was the size of a pumpkin and almost the same colour.

'Did you come in here to get out of the rain?' he asked. 'You should be home with your mummy and daddy. We can't have young girls out on the street alone at night. Are you after something other than a flannel to dry yourself off?'

'My dad is hitting my mum,' I whispered.

He leaned forward. 'I can't hear what you're saying. You'll need to speak up. A big voice, now.'

I put a hand to the side of my face, the same spot where my mother had been cut. 'He hit my mum with a plate and there's blood.'

'Your mother has been injured?' He frowned.

I nodded. 'He hurt her.'

He released a latch below the bench, lifted a section of the counter and stood directly in front of me. The policeman was a giant. 'You're telling me that your mother has been injured?' His size startled me and I became tongue-tied. 'What has happened?' he quizzed. 'You must tell me.'

'My mum. She's bleeding,' was all I could manage.

'Sarge,' he called.

An older policeman came over to the counter. He was bald, squat and grumpy-looking. They spoke in whispers and the giant policeman ordered me to follow him. When I wouldn't budge, fearful that I might be locked in one of the cells, he took my small hand in his paw and marched me through the station. He retrieved a black policeman's bike from a shed in the yard and ordered me to jump on the handlebars.

'I'll dink and you direct me, lass. Point the way home.'

I hitched my dress a second time and we rode through the streets in the rain, which were silent except for the slushing of bicycle tyres. I felt the policeman's warm breath on my neck and was reminded of my father. I shivered. As we turned into our street the policeman dismounted, lifted me from the handlebars and leaned the bike against Little Red's front fence. He hadn't spotted her waiting on the verandah for my return.

'Thank God. It's one of the Keystone boys.' Little Red chuckled into the darkness. 'We're saved.'

'Can I help you?' the policeman asked, unamused.

'Yes,' she said. 'You can help this girl and lock up that crazy man next door before he kills his own wife and the young one she has inside her.'

'You have some information on what has occurred next door?' he asked.

Little Red lit a match and held it towards the policeman to get a decent look at his face. 'Yes, I have information. As does that poor woman in that house. Information. It's here with this girl. Lift her dress, she'll have a story on her body to tell you. Women. Children. We carry our stories with us. Your job would be easy if you looked.'

'Don't tell me how to do my job,' he said. He took me by the hand. 'Let's see how your mother is.' He knocked at our front door and waited.

I heard my father's footsteps in the hallway, familiar, yet somehow uncertain. He opened the door. He'd stripped to his singlet and shorts. His permanently oiled hair was a mess. The anger on his face, looking down at me, was obvious.

'What?' he growled at the giant policeman, his chest lifting.

'Is this your daughter?' the policeman asked.

'She is.' My father reached across the doorway and grabbed me by the arm. 'Where have you been, Rose? Get inside.' He pulled me into the hallway and tried shutting the door.

The policeman wasn't having it. He planted a boot in the doorway. 'Your name, sir?'

'My name?' The anger in my father's voice was calculated to scare the officer away. A game of bullying and bluff that suited him.

'Yes. I need your name. I also need to know what has happened in your home tonight. I believe that your wife has been injured. That there has been an incident?'

I looked up at the policeman. For just a moment I thought he might be a hero.

'My name's Freddie Taylor. And there's been no incident here. Not in my house.' My father glared at the policeman.

The rain had stopped falling. Water rushed along the bluestone gutter in front of the house. The policeman remained calm and put a hand to the front door. 'I need to come inside, Mr Taylor, and speak with your wife personally.'

'No-one needs to do that,' my father said, pushing me lightly in the back, towards the kitchen.

'I'll decide that. Not you,' the policeman said.

He forced his way past my father, who followed him into the kitchen, calling anxiously, 'You don't need to speak with her. She has nothing to say to police.'

The earlier carnage had been swept away and the floor washed clean. My mother was sitting at the kitchen table, a bloodied towel pressed to the side of her face. Her free hand, resting on a knee, was shaking furiously. My father's trouser belt lay on the table, the brass buckle he regularly polished gleamed under the bare lightbulb above the kitchen table.

'Mrs Taylor?' the policeman asked.

If she heard what he said, it didn't seem to register with her. My mother looked at me with such fear on her face that I understood in that instant, it had been a mistake to take the advice of Little Red and run to the police station for help.

'You've obviously been hurt, Mrs Taylor. I need to look at

your injury.' The policeman kneeled beside Mum and took the towel away from her face, exposing the gash on her cheek. The bleeding had eased, but the cut was ugly.

'You will need to go to the hospital and have that seen to,' he said. 'It will need stitching.' He looked over his shoulder at my father, who was standing with his hands on his hips, staring with menace at my mother. The policeman stood up. He towered over my father. 'I need to know what's happened here tonight. The whole story.'

None of us spoke. My mother's foot nervously tapped the floor. She eventually broke our complicit silence. 'It was me,' she said. 'I had an accident.'

'An accident?' the policeman said, shaking his head. I could see he had immediately resigned himself to a performance he was familiar with.

'It was me,' she repeated. 'I was working here in the kitchen and the floor was wet after I'd mopped it, and I slipped. I hit my face on the corner of the table.'

The policeman examined the rounded edge of the kitchen table and turned to my father. 'What do you have to say, Mr Taylor?'

My father actually smiled. 'What can I say? My wife's clumsy. She always has been. Haven't you, love?' He walked over to my mother and rested a hand in the centre of her back. She grimaced. 'You're right, officer,' he said. 'I best get her to the hospital and have her taken care of.' He retrieved his shirt from the back of the kitchen chair and slipped it on. 'I'll show you out. We'll need to get going.'

The policeman looked around the room. His eyes settled

on a wedding photograph of my parents, framed on a wall. My mother was wearing the white gown she'd hastily borrowed from a friend. My father, sporting a dark pinstripe suit, had already faded into the background.

'You are about to have another child?' the policeman asked.

'Yes,' she answered. 'Soon.'

'Well, you can't afford accidents like this, as you call it, and endanger your baby's life.' He turned to my father. 'Your wife needs to be taken care of.'

'And she will be,' my father answered, buttoning his shirt. 'She will be. I'll show you out.'

'Don't bother. I'll show myself out.'

My father didn't take Mum to the hospital that night. He washed and dressed the cut before explaining in a perfectly calm voice, 'You'll be fine, this scratch will look after itself.'

Later that night my father came into the bedroom and woke me. 'Rose, come into the kitchen with me.' He marched me along the hallway, sat me at the kitchen table and quietly explained that *we* did not go to the police – or anybody else we might think of. We did not open our mouths to strangers about our private business, *family business*, he stressed.

The drunkenness and anger from earlier in the night had left him. My father had returned to a state of precision and order. He stroked my cheek. 'Do you understand me, Rose?'

I refused to answer. My defiance was obvious. He picked his trouser belt up from the table, slowly ran the leather strap through his hand and fondled the brass buckle. 'Do you understand?' he repeated. 'I won't ask again.'

I looked down at the belt buckle. He'd hit me with it before, erratically, drunkenly, without reason. I knew my father well enough to be certain that regardless of any answer I provided, the onslaught would not be avoided. The pair of us, we both knew that. My mother, lying awake in fear in the front room, she knew that. My little brother, Sean, a month away from life, he already knew it. Our next-door neighbour, Little Red, she knew. As did the giant policeman. We all knew. Our family secret was everyone's secret.

It had started raining again, the heavy drops beating on the kitchen roof. I remembered the words of my grandmother, dead two years, that 'rain on the roof is the song of a loving home'.

Well, not in our home.

'Take your pyjamas off,' my father ordered. I stripped to my underwear and turned away from him, just as my mother had.

'Look at me, Rose,' he said. 'You must look at me. I'm your father.'

I did look at him. I was nine years old. Ten at Christmas. I was as skinny as a rake and I was his daughter. In that moment I understood that our relationship was about to change. From that night onward, I would always refuse him.

My father spent the following week conjuring his next move. There was no smashing of plates, no trouser belts or flying fists. He sat at the table each night brooding, looking across the table at my mother and her pregnant stomach with a dark, dark face.

My body had remained bruised and tender from where my father had whipped me with the belt. My legs were covered in welts. It was decided that I would be kept away from school until they healed. Mum wouldn't let me out of her sight, worried I'd go out into the street and people would see my cuts and bruises, which didn't make a lot of sense, as many of us carried similar injuries to school, to church and to the shops, and nobody said a word about it.

She remained her timid self with him, and took her anger out on me. She found the housework increasingly difficult to manage, although she could never have met the standards demanded by my father. I helped her around the house, peeling vegetables, setting his dinner place at the table and cleaning up after him. Mum was as disappointed with my efforts at housework as he was with hers.

'Not that way,' she screamed at me one afternoon, watching me like a hawk as I cut the potatoes for his weekly roast dinner. She picked up a piece of raw potato and held it in front of my face. 'This is too small. I've told you. The potatoes break up in the roasting tray if they've been cut too small. Do you want to set him off?'

I turned away, frightened that she was about to hit me. 'No, Mum.'

She threw the potato in the bin. 'You learn from me or be drilled by him. It's your choice, girl.'

When the day arrived for Mum to have her final pregnancy check-up at the hospital, she demanded I go with her, and that I wear a pair of heavy winter tights and long sleeves, even though it was a warm day. We sat in the waiting room at the hospital, Mum nursing her belly and chewing her fingernails, me observing the other women in the scrubbed-clean cavernous room.

Some of the women were much younger than Mum. Others were older. I closely studied each of their faces. The older ones looked tired and kept to themselves, while the younger women appeared excited about being pregnant and spoke to each other just as loudly as they might sitting at a cafe drinking coffee. One woman, one of the older ones seated directly opposite Mum, nervously fingered a wedding band. I watched as she removed the ring and returned it several times to her finger. She and Mum lifted their heads simultaneously, a matching pair looking into a mirror – exhaustion, swollen stomachs and darkened eyes – before quickly turning away from the sight they'd been exposed to.

Mum's turn came to see the doctor and I followed her into the cubicle. The elderly doctor had eyebrows as bushy as the silver-haired man who read the news on the TV of a night. He frowned. 'I think it would be best if the child remains outside,' he said. 'This will be a physical examination, Mrs Taylor.'

'She stays here,' my mother snapped, before regaining some composure. 'Rose is a bit of a wanderer. I need to keep her in my sight.'

He pulled a blue curtain across the cubicle, darkening the room.

Mum dutifully answered the doctor's questions. He put a thermometer in her mouth, ordered her to unbutton her blouse and placed a stethoscope between her breasts, which were bursting out of a frayed brassiere. Listening to her heartbeat, he moved closer and studied the cut on her cheek. Mum turned away in an effort to hide the damaged side of her face.

15

'What happened to your cheek?' he asked.

'An accident,' she said, giving nothing away. He looked over at me, attempted a smile but failed.

He asked her to remove her underpants and lie on her back on a narrow table. He reached one hand under the table and I heard a clicking sound. The doctor lowered the bottom half of the table, then sat down on a round metal chair. Just as quickly he stood and adjusted the height of the chair by spinning the seat. When he sat down again, he opened a drawer at the side of the table and took out a pair of gloves.

'There is no need to be nervous, Mrs Taylor, we have done this before. Please lift your dress above your waist. Let's see if this baby is getting ready to show itself.'

The doctor's gloved hand reached between my mother's heavy legs. She arched her back slightly. Fearful of what I was witness to, I took my school shoes off and concentrated on tying and re-tying the laces until the examination was over.

'It won't be long now, I expect,' the doctor said, after completing the examination.

We were about to leave when he called Mum back into the cubicle. 'Your injury,' he said, 'the cut and bruising under your eye. If you wish it, I can make an appointment for you to speak with the social worker. A woman,' he added.

'There's no need,' Mum said, abruptly. 'I'm fine.'

After two weeks at home I was finally able to escape to the schoolyard. Each morning I'd walk to the bottom of the street and across the empty lot behind the bank building on the next corner. Then I'd jump the fence, cut through a laneway and exit opposite the school gate.

On my second day back, I spilled a jar of red paint over my tunic and white shirt in art class.

'What trouble are you up to now, Rose Taylor?' Sister Agnes scolded. 'Look at yourself. You've spoiled your school uniform. You need to take that tunic off now. Go to the washroom and scrub it.'

I did as I was told and started to take my tunic and shirt off, forgetting that my body still carried faint welts on my shoulders and back. Sister Agnes saw the markings, took me by the arm and whispered, 'Not in here. Do not remove your clothing in the classroom. Leave now and clean yourself in the washroom.' Some of the other girls giggled. 'Stop that!' Sister Agnes demanded, slapping her hands together. 'Go,' she said to me. 'And you come back here. Quickly.'

In the bathroom I scrubbed the red paint from my hands, removed my tunic and shirt, rinsed both in the sink and put my uniform back on, damp. Looking at myself in the mirror, I noticed a dark smudge across the bib of my tunic, above my heart. My face wore an equally dark expression. It matched my father's, and had appeared the morning after his last punishment. Even at such a young age I knew that I would never be entirely rid of it.

I left the toilets and raced from the schoolyard back along the laneway, scaling the fence behind the bank. I had an hour to wait before the end of the school day when I could go home, so I climbed the old peppercorn tree in the empty lot and sat high in its branches, out of sight, where I had a good view of our street. I thought about the new baby and couldn't imagine that my mother was ready for it. Or that my father would want it around the house at all.

A cat tightrope-walked along the top of the fence, spying me out of one eye before disappearing into a clump of blackberry thorn. He'd obviously escaped the clutches of Little Red, I thought. A moment later I saw her, walking along the street below me. Perhaps she'd been tracking the cat? I jumped down from the tree and crept out of the deserted lot. Little Red took little, quick steps. I followed her on the other side of the street, trapped between not wanting her to see me and, for a reason I didn't quite understand, wanting to speak to her again. She stopped outside her house, turned and waved at me to cross the street.

'I saw you up in the tree back there,' she said, opening her front door. 'Come into the house, before your mother sees you.'

I followed Little Red inside. The house smelled of the same scent she carried on her clothes and body. She pulled on a light cord and the narrow hallway lit up. The walls were papered with old newspapers. I stopped and read the headlines and looked at the photographs. Pictures of large boats, horses racing on the track, a truck lying on its side in a ditch after an accident. There was also a girl around my own age standing in the middle of a street. She wore rags for clothes and the buildings surrounding her were in ruin. I gazed into her eyes, which I would have expected to be sad. She looked back at me fiercely, as if to tell me, *Don't you stare at me*. I quickly turned away.

Little Red, who'd been watching me, rested a finger on the

photograph. 'I was once a girl like this. In another time. A place far from here.'

'Is that why you did this?' I asked. 'Papered the walls.'

'No. I found it this way when I moved here. The landlord was an Assyrian man, well-mannered he was. Just like you, kid. He opened the front door on the day I came to the house and said to me, "I'm sorry, missus, the man before, he was crazy. An artist. They are all crazy." He told me that if I wanted to live in the house he would paint over the news pages. I stopped him. "You cannot paint over history," I told him. I now have all these stories from around the world. They give me company.'

I looked back at the walls. 'Have you read all of these stories? Some of them look sad. This picture of the girl does. She's lost her home.'

'And what is wrong with sad stories? The world is always sad. This world, you must be ready for it, brave girl. You must understand that,' she said, kindly.

I didn't understand Little Red at all, not that afternoon, standing in her hallway. And I had no idea why she would call me brave. We'd spoken only once and all I had done was run to the police station, and that had been the wrong thing to do.

She pointed to the cornice above the front door. 'I have a stepladder in the yard that I used to drag in here, to climb up to these dark corners with a torch in my hand. Even up there are important stories. Not now. I'm too old to climb. But you can do it for me, read all these stories.'

The task seemed impossible. 'There must be a hundred stories here,' I said.

She waved dismissively. 'Many more than that. The stories begin in this room with the sinking of the *Titanic*, the big, big ship, with so many people, and end in the back room with the bomb. Boom! Boom! On the Japanese people.'

One sheet of newspaper carried a list of people's names printed above religious words. 'What are these for?' I asked.

'Obituaries. These are the names of people who have died and the prayers to send them away with.'

'Old people?'

'Some,' she said. 'But not all. See this one child,' she said. She put a fingernail to a name, lightly tapped it and read the inscription.

Baby Hannah – taken from our care – a gift to God.

She quickly became angry. 'A gift to God. Rubbish! No God would kill a child.'

'You don't believe in God?' I asked.

She threw the question back at me. 'Do you?'

'I don't know.'

'Well,' she said, 'you pray to God to save you and your mummy and the baby coming, you will be waiting a long time.'

I'd never heard anyone talk in such a way. It was true. Little Red had to be a witch.

She nodded in the direction of each room as she led me along the hallway. 'I sleep in this one at the front of the house. This second room is for guests, not that they come.' She laughed.

Both rooms were also lined with newspapers from floor to ceiling. The back room of the house, the kitchen, was a wonderful surprise. One wall was pasted with newspaper articles, although the decoration came to a halt halfway along the room.

The remaining walls were painted a soft blue colour and a floral-patterned lampshade hung from the low ceiling above the table. The room was cosily warm and crowded with small glass animal ornaments along a shelf, stacks of books resting against the walls and vases full of bright cloth flowers. Hundreds of flowers.

I touched one of the flowers in a vase on the table. 'You like that one?' she said. 'It is a rose. Just like you.'

'Where did you get all the flowers?' I asked.

'From the cemetery.'

I quickly withdrew my hand.

She detected a look of disapproval on my face. 'Don't you look at me that way. The flowers on the graves I leave to the dead. The ones that blow across the cemetery and get trapped in the iron spikes of the fence, they are mine. I bring them home and wash the dust away. They are happy here.'

She pointed to a chair. 'Sit at the table.' She took two glasses down from a shelf, reached into her pocket and pulled out a flask. 'Rum.' She smiled and poured a generous amount from the flask into a glass and placed the flask on the table. She then shuffled over to an ice-chest next to the stove and brought out a larger flask, which she poured into the second glass. The liquid was pink in colour.

'Drink this,' she said.

'What is it?' I asked, hesitating.

She slapped a hand lightly on the table. 'Ah! So, you think I'm going to poison you? It's tea. Rose tea. Just like you. Just like the flowers in the vase. Try.'

The only tea I'd ever drunk was a dull brown colour, with milk and sugar. I sniffed at the glass, picked it up and took a sip.

The tea was cold, and not so sweet as the cup I was used to. I savoured the taste on my tongue and took a second sip from the glass.

Little Red opened a packet of cigarettes and put one in her mouth. 'You sure you won't smoke?' she asked.

I couldn't understand why a grown-up would want me to smoke a cigarette. 'No, thank you.'

She lit the cigarette, drew on it contentedly and sat back in the chair. 'I know that you all think I'm a witch. I hear the songs of the children. Tell me the truth. Do you believe that I am a witch?' she added. 'And please, drink your tea.'

I took a deep breath before answering. 'Well, some of the kids say that you used to be in the circus. Or that you're a gypsy.' I took another deep breath. 'And they do say you're a witch, that you can cast spells on people, and ... and ... you murder cats.'

'Murder cats!' Little Red threw her head back and laughed. 'Oh, that is good. Murder cats. I have not heard that story before. Why cats?'

'It was after some of the cats went missing,' I said. 'People say you killed them all.'

Little Red shook her head. 'I would never kill a cat, not unless I was starving. I would have killed one back in the war. And eaten it. But not now. Do you know why there are no cats left here, Rosie?'

I had no idea. 'Why?'

'Because they are cowards. They watched and did nothing and the rats got bigger.' She reached a hand across the table and rested her open hand on my chest. 'You see a rat, Rosie, you kill it early and kill it hard. Otherwise, you make trouble for yourself.'

She took a decent mouthful of rum. 'What else do they say about me out there in the street,' she asked, a glint in her eye.

'Well …' I looked around the room a little nervously before answering. 'Some people say that you have a toilet inside your house.'

Little Red got up, opened a door behind the kitchen, turned the light on and stood back. I'd never seen a more impressive room. The floor was laid with sparkling white tiles and the toilet was also white, *porcelain*, with a varnished wooden seat.

I took a sip of my beautiful rose tea, still in my hand. 'Does it work?' I asked.

'You watch,' Little Red said. For a moment I thought she might lift her dress and drop her underpants, as my mother had done at the hospital, but instead she pulled the brass chain hanging from the cistern. Together we looked down and watched the clear water create a whirlpool in the toilet bowl.

'Do you like it?' she asked.

'I think it's lovely,' I said.

'Would you like to try it for yourself?' she said.

'I beg your pardon?'

'The toilet. Would you like to have a wee-wee? Or whatever else?'

My mother had brought me up to never use any toilet but our own, to protect myself from germs, she said, which didn't make a lot of sense, seeing as our toilet was infested with rats and never worked properly. When I was desperate to go to the toilet at school, Mum told me that I should squat on the seat.

Not that I ever did. Such a feat was difficult, and I feared I might tumble into the bowl.

I wanted nothing more at that moment than to sit on Little Red's toilet. 'Are you sure it's okay?' I asked.

She clicked her fingers. 'Hand me the glass, kid. We do not drink tea on the toilet.'

I closed the door, lifted my dress, clenched the hem between my teeth and slid my undies below my knees. The toilet seat was warm and smooth. There was none of the bad smells of our outdoor toilet on account of the broken pipes. I took the slowest wee I could, not wanting my stay to end. I wondered if rich people had toilets so immaculate. I stood, pulled my undies up, flushed and watched. I washed my hands in an equally sparkling basin and flushed the toilet one more time.

I opened the door. 'I've finished.'

Little Red filled my glass with more tea and placed her hand on mine. 'When your father goes crazy, do you hide? When I was a girl I also ran and hid from men.'

'I do have hiding places,' I said. 'But he's found most of them.'

She noticed the tears in my eyes and jumped up from the table. She took a tea towel from the sink and gently wiped my face. 'Are you afraid?' she said. 'Don't be afraid. You are a brave girl.'

But I was very afraid that when the baby was born my father would hurt it, even kill the baby. She sat back down. I looked closely at Little Red's face, into her striking blue eyes.

'What is it?' she asked.

'Can you make spells?' I whispered.

She leaned across the table. 'What sort of spells?'

'Ober … ober rituals?'

'You mean obituaries?' she said, even more quietly.

I couldn't speak and nodded instead. She rested back in her chair and smiled. 'So, you want me to cast a spell? A death spell? On who?'

'My father.'

'I see.'

I thought she might scold me, but she didn't.

She got up from the kitchen table, opened a drawer and brought out a pencil and notebook. 'Here. You write your father's name. You must write it, not me. Write his full name.'

I wrote my father's name, *Frederick Francis Taylor*, in the neatest hand I could manage.

The spell was cast quicker than I would have imagined. Little Red tore the name from the notepaper, placed it in an empty Vegemite jar, put a match to it and uttered a few words in a language I couldn't understand. I watched as a thin column of smoke wafted above the table.

'Put a finger in the jar,' she said.

'My finger? But it's hot.'

She pursed her lips and blew gently into the jar. 'Not now. Put a finger in the jar. Collect the ash.'

I did as she told me. My finger warmed but didn't burn.

'Take it out now,' she said.

I examined the dark smudge on my fingertip. It reminded me of the stained cross of Ash Wednesday, smeared on the foreheads of churchgoers.

'Taste it,' Little Red said.

'Taste it?'

'Yes. Put your finger in your mouth and taste the ash.'

Again I did as she said. As soon as my fingertip touched my tongue I felt a shiver in my body. She watched my reaction closely. 'Good. It is done.'

'Is that it?' I asked.

'It is,' she said, rubbing her hands together. 'It is done.'

'What happens now?'

'It is up to you, brave girl. If you truly believe, fate is what will happen. Fate for you and fate for the baby.'

I stared up as the final curl of smoke wafted above our heads. I didn't really know what the word fate meant, but was too shy to ask. 'Thank you, Little Red,' I said, yet to understand what I was thankful for.

'Ach! In this house, me and you together, I am not Little Red.'

'What should I call you?'

'By my name, Sophia.' I loved the sound *Sophia* made when she spoke the word. 'You must go now,' she said, surprising me by giving me a hug. My mother never hugged or kissed me. She walked me to the front door, held my hand and said, 'Take care, Rosie.'

My father sat at the kitchen table that night, having not spoken a word since coming through the front door after work. The house appeared to sense his presence – I was certain I could feel it shaking. I was ready to hide if needed.

My mother had cooked his favourite meal, roast chicken. 'I've done you extra stuffing,' she said, placing a dinner plate in front of him and retreating to the sink. He picked up the knife and gripped it so tightly his knuckles turned white. My mother looked across the room at him and he stared at her stomach. He cut fiercely into the chicken and shoved a large portion of meat into his mouth. I watched him closely, chewing at the meat.

'It's undercooked,' he said, jabbing the air with his knife. 'The meat's pink and bloody.'

Mum wrung her hands together and shook in time with the house. She tried to reason with him. 'No. I gave it ten minutes extra, Fred, because I know that's how you like it.'

He tore a leg from the carcass and held it in the air. 'Look!' he screamed. 'Look, woman!'

But Mum wouldn't look. She held both hands to her stomach and stared at me, as if pleading for me to do something. He was about to throw the meat across the room but changed his mind and crammed the entire chicken leg into his mouth, followed by a handful of stuffing.

I heard the sound of breaking bone. He chewed on the leg a little longer and then he did something odd, for my father at least. He seemed to smile over at the two of us, his mouth stuffed with meat, greasy skin and splintered bones.

My father's face was always a blackish colour, on account of his permanent state of anger, so I didn't notice the change in his cheeks until he suddenly dropped his knife. He lifted a hand in the air as if he was hailing a taxi, and reached for his throat. It was the strangest thing I had ever seen. He soon had both hands wrapped around his throat, as if he was about to choke himself. He coughed and spluttered and spat grizzled meat onto the wooden table.

Mum froze. We both did.

'What's happening to him?' I said to Mum.

'I'm not sure yet,' she answered, calmly.

It wasn't until he fell from the chair onto the floor that either of us was able to move. I involuntarily jumped up onto my chair. 'What should we do?' I asked her.

Mum was silent. We looked down at him. His face had turned a deep bruised colour, just like the black eyes he had given my mother and the colour of the welts on my body after he'd whipped me with the trouser belt. His eyes were bulging, pleading with her. His legs kicked and his workboots slammed against the floorboards. I heard a second sound coming from his mouth, beneath the frenzied cough. It was just like the sound of air slowly being released from a tyre.

'What is it?' I asked again, unable to move from the chair.

Mum stood above him and rested her weary arms on her hips. 'I think it might be a chicken bone,' she said. 'The wish bone.'

AFTER LIFE

MY YOUNGER BROTHER, BILLY, LIVED in the same one-bedroom flat on a government housing estate for twenty years. A street of identical two-storey buildings had been constructed from interlocking concrete panels and painted in chequerboard pink and green pastels. The colours were chosen as they apparently calmed anxious people. A few short years after the estate opened, which came complete with a ribbon-cutting ceremony and a brass plaque, the complex developed a terminal condition described by an engineer as 'concrete cancer'. The walls blistered and eroded at the corner panels, while the variety of pastels faded to a uniform grey-green. Two decades later the same walls were covered in graffiti tags, consisting of abstract hieroglyphics with no meaning to anyone but the offenders themselves.

Until a month ago, when I spent time there twice in the space of a couple of weeks, I hadn't been inside Billy's flat for over two years. On that second occasion my younger sister,

Angie, had called and asked if I would help her clean the flat. I felt uneasy about returning again and argued with my sister.

'Why the rush, Ange? We can do this a bit later.'

'No, we can't, Joe. It's a Commission estate.'

'What's that got to do with it?' I asked, although I knew exactly what Angie meant.

'With nobody there to look after the place, someone will break in and rob it. You know. Thieves.'

'Come on,' I moaned. 'Billy wasn't robbed once in all the years he lived there.'

'Only because he never went out and had it locked up like Fort Knox. He wouldn't let anyone in. Even family.' She softened her voice. 'Please, Joe? I can't do this without your help. I want to clear it out. What we don't want we can give to the Salvation Army. It could be fun.'

'Fun? What sort of fun would it be, Angie?'

'I don't know. Sorry, I don't even know why the fuck I said that. All I know is I need you, Joe. Please.'

'Alright. I'll meet you there in the morning.'

The next day I rode my bike across the city. When I got to Billy's flat, Angie was on her hands and knees cleaning the bathroom floor with a bucket of hot water, a scrubbing brush and what smelled like ammonia.

'What's this, trauma cleaning?' I said, before realising. 'Sorry, Ange.'

'You don't have to apologise to me, Joe. You found him.'

She dropped the scrubbing brush back into the bucket,

slowly stood up and grabbed hold of her lower back. 'God, my back is fucked. Never get pregnant, Joe. It's joy for a day and misery for life.'

'You don't need to do this,' I said, following her into the kitchen. 'The Housing Commission will come in and clean before the new tenant takes over.'

'You think I'm doing this to save the Commission? Or for the next tenant? Fuck the Commission, Joe. Billy couldn't get them around here to fix a leaky tap. I'm doing this for us. For him.'

'How's that, Ange?'

She poked me in the chest. 'Mum scrubbed this flat clean the day before we moved him in here. We'll be leaving it the same way. We're clean people, Joe. I won't have anyone badmouthing our brother.'

'You should have been a social worker,' I teased.

She removed the cleaning gloves from her hands and filled the kettle. 'You want coffee?'

'Instant?' I frowned.

'Get over your snobbery, Joe. There was a time when it was a luxury in our house, when we were kids.' She picked up the jar. *Maxwell House.* 'It won't poison you,' she said, spooning the coffee into two mugs. 'And are you going to help clean or not? You're not here to hand out advice. If you don't want to help, please jump on your bike and pedal home. I can't have you standing around watching me.'

'Don't kick off. I'll help. After a cup of your special blend.'

Angie filled the mugs with hot water and milk and nodded in the direction of Billy's bedroom. 'But before we start, you have to show me how you found him.'

I could hardly believe what she'd said. 'What do you mean?'

'I need to see where he was in the bedroom when you found him.' She walked into Billy's room.

I refused to follow her. 'I'm not doing it, Angie. I can't.'

She turned around, came back to where I was standing and took hold of my hand. Burying her face in my woollen jumper, she whispered, almost inaudibly, 'I'm sorry.'

I had always melted when my younger sister really needed me. I placed a hand gently on the back of her head. 'Sorry for what, Angie? You've done nothing wrong.'

'But I did, Joe. I made certain that you would be the one to find him. I was too afraid to come over here.'

'But you couldn't have.'

'I did, Joe. I took the call from his nurse, Paul. He told me that he'd found Billy *unresponsive*. He didn't say he was dead. But I knew. Straightaway, I knew. I didn't have the courage to be with my own brother.' She began to sob and gripped my hand tighter. 'That's why I called you, Joe. I couldn't do it. I'm so sorry.'

Together we went into Billy's bedroom. The mattress had been stripped. Taking a deep breath, I pointed to the floor at the end of the bed. The dark bloodstain in the carpet was obvious. 'Here. I found him lying here.'

Angie wiped her eyes on the sleeve of her jumper. 'Where, exactly?' she asked.

'Well, his feet were at this corner of the bed and he was lying on his side.'

Angie lay down on the floor and turned on her side. 'Like this?'

'Why are you doing this, Angie?'

'Like this?' she repeated, insistently.

'Yeah, like that,' I said.

Lying on her side, Angie opened her hand and lightly clawed at the carpet with her fingertips. She then curled her body into a ball and closed her eyes. I sat on the bed and breathed in and out quietly, in unison with my sister. She eventually got up from the floor, sat next to me and draped an arm around my shoulders. Neither of us spoke.

We began by tidying in the bedroom, packing Billy's belongings, of sentimental value or otherwise, into cardboard boxes. After an hour of sorting we'd filled only one box with the things we wanted to keep – a few old photographs and books, two crucifixes and the scapular Billy had been wearing around his neck when he died. Angie sat the open box on the kitchen table. 'Not much to show for a life,' she said, her eyes watering.

I picked up a photograph of the three of us together as kids, in a park nearby the house we grew up in. In the photo Angie is seated to one side of Billy, me on the other. His head of luscious curls dominates the photograph.

'Look, Joe, this is so beautiful,' she said.

'What is?'

'You. Look at the way you have your arm around Billy's shoulder, looking out for him. You always took care of your brother.'

'Did I?'

She kissed me on the cheek. 'Yes, you did.'

Once we'd finished in the bedroom I opened a cupboard above the stove in the kitchen and discovered Billy's black duffel coat, neatly folded, inside a shopping bag.

'Look at this.' I unfolded the coat. 'Billy's good duffel coat.'

'You should put it on,' she said.

I felt uneasy at the suggestion. 'I can't do that.'

'Of course, you can. Put it on. For me. Please.'

I slipped the coat on and was surprised at how immediately comforted I felt wearing it. Angie straightened the collar and buttoned the wooden buttons. Her actions conjured a memory of our mother doing the same for me when I was a young boy about to leave the house for school on a cold winter's morning.

'It looks so good on you. You have to take it home with you.'

'You think I should?'

'Of course, Joe. This coat needs to be worn and I can't imagine it on the back of a stranger.'

Angie emptied the sideboard and, wearing the duffel coat, I sorted through the cupboards in the kitchen, stacking plates, cups and glasses on the kitchen bench. I lifted a rice cooker out of the cupboard and placed it on the bench. The cord was badly frayed. 'The Salvos won't take this,' I said, showing her the damaged cord. 'I'll put it out with the rubbish.'

I walked through the laundry and out to an open yard behind the block of flats where the oversized wheelie bins were kept. A silver-haired man wearing a nylon jacket over grey trackpants and a stained white T-shirt was emptying rubbish into one of the bins. I opened the lid of another one.

'You don't want that?' he asked.

'No. The cord's damaged, it could be dangerous.'

'Do you mind if I have a look at it?' I handed the cooker to him. 'I reckon I can fix this,' he said. 'We might have a spare cord in the men's shed.'

'The men's shed?'

'Yeah. We have one on the estate, although ours has never been a men-only affair. We open it to anyone – men, women, kids. All-comers, on or off the estate. We've got spare parts for just about any electrical appliance you can think of. You wouldn't believe what people throw out.'

'What do you do with them?' I asked.

'We repair what we can and help people out. Toasters. Microwave ovens. And now, rice cookers.' He laughed, then took a packet of cigarettes and a box of matches from his jacket pocket. 'I'm Mick, by the way. You like a smoke?'

I looked from the packet of smokes to his nicotine-stained teeth. 'No thanks, Mick.' I offered my hand. 'I'm Joe.'

Mick seemed to be studying me. 'Do you have a flu, mate?'

'No. Why?'

'That coat. You must be warm in that.'

'It belongs to my brother,' I said, which didn't really explain why I was wearing it on such a warm day. 'We might have some other electrical gear you might want,' I offered. 'I'm clearing out my brother's flat, with my sister.'

'Oh,' he said, knowingly. 'That would be Billy's place?'

'Yes. He was … he is my brother.'

'I'm really sorry about what happened,' he said. 'Billy was a gentle man.'

'You knew him?' I asked, surprised.

'We all knew Billy.'

'I thought he hardly left home, except to go to the shops. I didn't know that anyone knew him.'

'He was quiet, your brother. Didn't say much. But at least once a week he'd come by the shed, sometimes dropping off a find he'd come across when he was out walking. He'd sit and have a morning cuppa too, now and then.'

'A morning cuppa?'

'Yep. And biscuits. Cakes if one of the women on the estate was in the mood to bake.'

I tried imagining Billy sitting in a room of people enjoying a cup of tea. It wasn't easy.

Mick noticed the puzzled look on my face. 'Like I said, he didn't say much except "thank you" when he left the shed. Some of the others, they don't have any more to say than he did. We don't fuss over that. It's not as if it's speech night at the town hall.'

'Do you want to come and see if there's anything else you want from the flat?' I offered.

'I'd like that. Yeah.'

I took Mick into the flat and introduced him to Angie. 'This is Mick. He repairs stuff. He's going to fix the cord on the rice cooker. I've been telling him that maybe some other stuff here might be of value. For the shed.'

'The shed?' Angie asked.

'The men's shed,' I said, as if I was already familiar with it.

'I'm really sorry about your brother,' Mick said to Angie. 'We liked him.'

'We?' Angie asked, as surprised as I'd been.

'Most of us on the estate. Except for a few who keep to themselves. What are you planning to give away?' he asked, looking around the room.

'All of it,' she said, 'except that cardboard box on the bench.'

'The furniture?' he asked.

'Yep. All of it,' she repeated.

He whistled. 'I'll be back in a few minutes.'

Angie and I dragged a pair of chairs into the street and sat drinking more instant coffee. We watched on as people carried goods out of the flat. Before any of the neighbours entered Billy's place, they approached us and offered condolences. Some became tearful as they spoke. Each time someone left the flat with a piece of furniture, a stack of plates or a bag of spare linen, they would stop and check if it was okay with us first.

Eventually, the flat was empty and Mick thanked us again. 'You've been generous. Billy, too. You come by the shed for a visit one day, the two of you.'

'Did Billy ever mention any of these people to you?' Angie asked, after Mick had left.

'No, but there wasn't much he did mention.'

We sat quietly for a few minutes, neither of us speaking. 'I should go,' I said at last. 'I'll lock up.'

We hugged each other, then Angie picked up the cardboard box of saved belongings. I reached into it and retrieved the photograph we'd been looking at earlier and put it in a pocket of the coat.

I locked Billy's door behind us and was about to jump on my bike and ride home when I noticed a jade plant sitting on the front porch. I'd never seen a plant that looked so close to death. I pulled it out of its pot and shook the dried lumps of clay from the roots. I held it in one hand and straddled the bike.

'You're not going to take that coat off?' Angie said. 'You'll pass out from heat stress before you get home.'

'You told me that it suits me. I'm leaving it on for a bit longer.'

'Wait,' Angie said. She kissed me on the tip of my nose. 'You look a little ridiculous, Joe. Billy would have laughed at you. You know, *that* gorgeous laugh he had when he was a kid.'

'Yeah, that laugh,' I said. 'It was so beautiful.'

Pedalling slowly home, I steered the bike with one hand and held the jade plant in the other.

Later that afternoon I placed the plant in an empty bucket, washed the dried clay away from its roots and carefully took some cuttings. They felt limp, absent of life. I found some plastic pots and a bag of soil in the shed and planted each one. With a watering can, I gently showered the cuttings. I then went into the house and put the kettle on. Waiting for the water to boil, I sat at the kitchen bench and held the photograph in one hand, studying Billy's joyous face. I made a cup of tea, went back outside and sat and waited for a garden to grow.

BOBBY MOSES

HUNTER DAY PARKED THE POLICE car on the side of the road under a two hundred year old ironbark. He left the engine humming with the aircon cranked to protect him from the blistering heat melting the bitumen outside. If his boss at the station, Reggie Booth, unexpectedly drove by Hunter could claim he was tracking the occasional passing vehicle with the station's radar gun. Except that the gun was faulty. A week earlier it had clocked a spluttering tractor at one hundred and forty clicks. Hunter held his mobile phone in one hand, scanning through images of Reggie's wife, Delores. She sent him a new photograph each morning, after she'd showered, but before she dressed. Their affair was six months old. Hunter didn't give a lot of thought to why it had started or what kept it going. He hated Reggie, which was reason enough.

Hunter heard the crunch of gravel and dropped the phone in his lap. 'Fuck me,' he croaked, looking out through the grubby front windscreen. An old blackfella was walking along the other side of the road towards him. He wore a dark suit and an Akubra hat slanted to one side, and carried a small pack on his back. As he passed the car, the Aboriginal man turned his head and glanced across the road in the policeman's direction. Once he'd passed, Hunter looked into the rear-view mirror and watched the old man closely for some time until his dark frame melded into the shimmering haze lifting from the road.

Hunter hadn't seen a blackfella this close to town for a long time. The last of the mission boys, Coalie Carter, had been dead six years. Coalie had lived until he was eighty-six, and had been as popular at the mine where he worked as he was among his own people. When he died the town turned out for him, and Aboriginal people – many of them, who like Coalie, had been born on the mission – came from all over the state to pay their respects and pray for his soul. The mob who came to see him off were gone as quickly as they'd arrived, much to the relief of local residents.

Standing out front of the police station the morning after the funeral, Reggie had turned and boasted to Hunter, 'With Coalie gone this is a totally white town now. Not a single boong to be seen above the ground.'

Hunter said nothing in reply, but he did smile to himself. *This may be a white town*, he thought, *but it's fucked*. The coal mine had shut down ten years earlier and the workers had moved on, chasing timber mostly. The town's businesses gradually went with them. Half of the shopfronts in the main streets had been whitewashed, while many of those left open were a final debt away from closing. With little in the way of serious crime, Hunter's police work was spent chasing sheep rustlers and dealing with the occasional drunk, who could neither afford to leave town nor tolerate being left behind without alcohol for company.

Hunter did a U-turn and drove back towards town. He passed the blackfella again, slowed the car and pulled into the side of the road up ahead. He got out, leaned against the bonnet and waited for the old man to reach him.

When he did, the old man stopped, straightened his hat and flicked the brim back with a fingertip, a gesture of courtesy. He knew well, through a life of hard lessons, there was no passing a copper on the side of an empty road without being questioned, most likely talked down to, and maybe given a belting if he put a single word out of place.

'How you doing?' Hunter said.

The old man took his hat from his head and looked the policeman in the eye, balancing deference with stubborn pride. 'Oh, I'm doing pretty good, I reckon.'

'Your name would be?' Hunter asked, lazily, as if he didn't really care for the answer.

'It would be Robert Moses. But I go by Bobby.'

Hunter Day knew the Moses surname well. Half the headstones in the cemetery carried the name Moses. It was shared by many Aboriginal people of the district, a remnant of the early mission days when Old Testament titles were doled out to blackfellas by the missionaries. Hunter brushed a fly from his sweating forehead, looked up at the noonday sky and then down at Bobby Moses. The thought of a total stranger

41

carrying a name so familiar unnerved him. He looked over Bobby's shoulder, back along the road.

'What brings you out this way?' Hunter asked. 'You heading for some place?'

Bobby lifted his chin. 'I'm heading for the town just along here. I got a ride along on the highway all the way from the city. Truck driver dropped me at the turn-off back a way, said I had maybe a two-hour walk left in me. I've just about covered that distance, I reckon.'

Hunter raised an eyebrow. 'You headed into our town? Stein?'

Bobby knew better than to say too much to the copper. He'd shared a cell with an old tribal fella, scarred up and all, who had been making his way across the desert when he was caught stealing from a petrol station. He hardly uttered a word to Bobby in the five months they were in lock-up together. The only advice he offered to Bobby before he got out was, 'More you talking, more trouble you make for yourself.'

'That's the town, alright,' Bobby answered. 'Stein. I'm here to catch up with my people.'

Hunter studied the old man's face. Bobby's leathered skin, tough, dark and wrinkled, carried a story of hard times. Hunter Day liked to think he had nothing against blackfellas. He hardly gave them a thought, one way or the other. He did know that his boss, and others in the town, wouldn't be happy seeing a black face around the streets again.

Hunter straightened up. He towered over Bobby. 'Stein is a small place, Mr Moses. I know your family name. But I can tell you that there's none of your people living here any longer. There's no-one to catch up with.'

'That could be so,' Bobby said, nodding his head. 'But I feel a need to set my eyes on the town. And the country. I feel a strong need inside me to see the country. That's the reason I've come by this way.'

Whatever Bobby Moses was after, Hunter was certain the townspeople wanted to keep the country to themselves. It wouldn't be a great day for Hunter either, if he didn't put a stop to the old man's wanderings. Reggie Booth would read the riot act to him for letting a blackfella loose on the streets of Stein.

Hunter stepped forward and pressed an open hand against Bobby's chest. Bobby looked down at the hand and back up at the policeman. 'So, you're related to the Aboriginal people from the mission?' Hunter said.

A crow landed on the roof of the police car and squawked at the policeman.

'That would be right,' Bobby said. 'People from their own country.'

'Well, most of your people are buried in the cemetery outside of town. And I'd think that walking in this heat takes it out of you. If you'd like to pay a visit to your people I'll drive you out to the cemetery myself. You can pay your respects and then …' Hunter licked his parched lips.

Bobby knew the copper was in a hurry for him to move on, but he wasn't about to. He was worn out after travelling hundreds of miles. The offer of an air-conditioned ride in a police car was tempting. He tipped his hat a second time. 'Thank you, boss. I'll take the ride.'

★

The pair didn't speak at all during the drive out to the cemetery. Hunter inspected the road ahead and Bobby concentrated on his long, wrinkled fingers. They turned off the road onto a winding gravel track.

'It's just up here over the ridge,' Hunter explained. 'Blackfellas have been buried here since the first years of the mission.'

Bobby said nothing and looked out the side window towards the hills in the distance. Hunter parked on one side of the cattle gate guarding the entrance to the cemetery. They got out of the car. The policeman gestured to the gate and walked behind Bobby, noticing that the old man carried a slight limp.

Bobby moved slowly between the rows of graves in the cemetery, pausing occasionally to read an inscription. Some of the graves were marked with traditional headstones or makeshift memorial cairns erected from broken house-bricks. Other graves were unmarked, while the details of some of the recently deceased had been roughly documented in black oil paint on the front of dented and scratched hub caps driven into the earth.

Hunter stood and watched as Bobby bowed his head at the foot of the grave of Eliza May Moses, who had been born on the mission over eighty years earlier.

'Do you know her?' Hunter asked, after Bobby had raised his head and walked from the grave.

Bobby turned to the policeman. 'Oh, I do. This is my own mummy in the ground right here.'

The date of the woman's death indicated that she'd been gone for fifty years. 'Your mother? When did you last see her?' Hunter asked.

Bobby was distracted, taking in country. He could *feel* it. 'Oh, I can't remember when that would be. When I was a newborn bub, well, I would have seen her then. Maybe I was put to her breast.' He shrugged. 'But I have no memory of that time either.'

Bobby headed back to the cemetery gate, lifting small swirls of dust in his wake. He opened the passenger door and got back into the police car. Hunter stayed where he was for a minute or two, looking down at the old man's footsteps, unsure of what he should say or do next.

Hunter climbed into the driver's seat and put the key in the ignition. He'd heard the stories about the old days when mission kids were hauled away to the religious homes, never to return, leaving behind wailing families and grieving mothers.

'You grow up with any of your own people?' he finally asked Bobby.

'Not one of them,' Bobby said. 'I could never find them. I didn't know my birth name until five years back, when I got hold of my Welfare Board file. My adopted name is Arthur. But my mum back there, I found out that she'd named me Robert.' He looked across at Hunter and smiled. 'I'm Bobby Moses. Her own boy.' A fly buzzed against the windscreen, erratically head-butting the glass. Bobby unwound the passenger-side window. 'How far is them mountains over there?'

'On foot, a good two-hour walk. A bit more. There's nothing out there. When they opened up the coal around here, the mining company believed there'd be a decent deposit under them hills. They did a few exploratory drills and came up with nothing.'

'That's my people's country,' Bobby said.

Hunter had heard about Aboriginal people further south making noises about land rights in the district. He looked at Bobby, wondering if he had an ageing agitator sitting next to him.

'What makes you think that?' he asked. 'You read about it in some city newspaper?'

'Nah,' Bobby scoffed. He put a hand to his heart. 'I know it.' He smiled at the policeman. Bobby wasn't certain why, but he felt that there might be something decent about Hunter. He'd come across plenty of bad coppers. Some of them mad too. But working out in the bush, away from the big cities and people, some police were lonely for company and would befriend just about anyone. Others took in the horizon every day and saw the country differently. Bobby wasn't sure where Hunter was coming from but thought he could take a chance on the young fella.

'I could walk out there,' he said. 'Or if you could see your way to drive me, I would be able to pay a visit to my country and then I'd be happy to be on my way again and leave you and your town in peace.'

Hunter turned the ignition key and revved the motor. The old man's offer would get him off the hook. 'I'll drive you. But we can't be out there for too long. I'll need to drop you back on the highway and get back to the station before it gets dark. Or I'll have my sergeant riding me.'

Bobby pressed his new acquaintance. 'Is he a bit of a bugger? Your boss?'

Hunter laughed. 'More like an arsehole.'

★

A little while later Hunter pulled off the road onto a red-dirt track and drove towards a rounded hill, topped with scraggy eucalypts. The track ended suddenly, at a stand of wattles.

'We're here,' Hunter said. 'What do you want to do now?'

'Well,' Bobby mused, scratching the bristles on his chin. 'I'm gonna need to get out here and take a walk.'

'A walk? Don't go too far. You might get lost.'

Bobby chuckled to himself. He wasn't about to get lost on his own country. He hopped out of the car, looked up at the sky briefly and down at the ground. Hunter watched as Bobby walked between a pair of gum trees and disappeared from sight, into the bush. He took his phone out of his jacket pocket. Delores had sent him another photograph of herself, holding a handwritten sign in front of her naked body. It read, I MISS U. Hunter smiled and flicked back through the catalogue of images.

A fierce wind buffeted the car, shifting it from side to side, followed by a thunderclap and the first heavy drops of rain. Hunter wound down the window to see if Bobby was heading back to the car. There was no sign of him.

For the next half-hour, Hunter listened to the rain and thunder as he tried composing a poem to text back to Delores. Lightning bolts momentarily lit the sky. When the rain finally eased he again wound down his window. The sight of the motionless shadow of the old man leaning against a tree frightened Hunter. Initially, it looked like Bobby Moses's body was hanging from a limb. Hunter jumped out of the car and walked towards the tree. Bobby was soaking wet. His dark suit clung to his frame and he was holding his shoes in one hand. His feet were covered in mud, twigs and eucalypt leaves.

'Where did you get to?' Hunter asked. 'You must be crazy, running around in the rain in bare feet.'

'Oh, I went crazy a long time ago. Years and years back.' Bobby laughed. 'I tell you something that sent me crazy,' he added, without any prompting from the police officer. 'When I got hold of my government file, I read that after I'd been taken from my mummy and put in the Home, white people came to look at me with the thought of taking me for their own. And all of them rejected me. Knocked me back.' Bobby laughed louder. 'Think how that would send you crazy,' he said. 'These bastards take you from your own people, claiming that your own mum is no good. And then none of these righteous cunts want you anyway.' Bobby walked past Hunter. 'Yep,' he said, opening the passenger door, 'reading that sent me crazy for a year or more.'

Hunter was taken aback, but he couldn't help but be drawn to Bobby. Righteous cunts! The town was full of them. He returned to the car.

Sitting inside, Bobby was putting his wet socks and shoes back on. 'We can go now,' he ordered.

'Where you off to next?' Hunter asked.

'I'm not sure,' Bobby said. 'If I can get a lift east, I'll head east. Or I'll go west. I haven't decided. See what turns up.'

'What did you see back there? In the bush?'

'Like I told you when you stopped me on the road: I wanted to see my people's country.'

'You didn't see much of it.'

Bobby coughed and wiped saliva from his mouth. 'I seen what I needed to. I'm gonna die soon. I have this cancer in my chest, the lungs. My wish was to stand on my country, feel my skin in the earth, breathe the air out this way, and hear the country and my old mum talking to me. I've done what was needed.'

Hunter stopped the car where the road met the highway. 'So, it could be east? Or it could be west?'

'Yep,' Bobby answered. 'Whichever ride I get. I'm not worried much now, where I end up.' He opened the door to get out of the car.

'Wait,' Hunter said. 'Wait. Hey, I can't leave you on the highway. Another storm could be coming. Let me put you up for the night.'

'And where would that be?' Bobby chuckled. 'In a police cell? That's a dangerous spot for a blackfella. Any fella. I'd be best taking my chances out here on the road. And besides, I've never liked them blankets you coppers have. Like sandpaper.'

'No,' Hunter said. 'Not at the station. I have a farmhouse out of town. The family farm. We lost the land years ago in the drought. But we hung on to the house. I can put you up.'

'Put me up?' Bobby frowned.

'Yeah. Put you up. You can stay out here and get soaked to the bone or get knocked to Shit Creek by a road train, or come home with me and have a shower and something to eat. And I've got a spare bed.'

'What about your bugger of a boss?' Bobby asked. 'Would he be happy about this?'

'Don't worry about Reggie. He's never happy. He won't be until he can get a transfer out of here, back to the city.'

'Okay,' Bobby said. 'You have a blanket for me?'

'Two.'

'They're not police issue?'

'Decent wool blankets. My wife bought them the week before she took off. Left them behind. I think she felt sorry for me.'

Bobby studied Hunter's face as he considered the offer. 'You're just a kid,' he whispered, as much to himself as the policeman. 'You have a fire at this farmhouse?'

'Yep. It's a beauty.'

'TV?'

'Yep.'

'Would you be able to bring me out here for another look in the morning?'

'If that's what you want,' Hunter said.

'Good. I need to see this country in the morning light. I reckon it will have more to say.'

BICYCLE THIEVES

JACK GARRETT RODE A BIKE to work for over thirty years. He laid hot mix with a road crew for the local council and his skin had been permanently baked, leaving him with the face of a battered football. Road work was thirsty, summer and winter. Jack would go to the pub once he'd knocked off for the day and, a couple of hours later, he'd set his old black bike to autopilot and let it guide him home.

The day after he retired from the council, he walked the bike down the street to our house and knocked at the door.

'Is your mum in?' he asked.

'Nup. She's on afternoon shift.'

The old bike was resting against the light pole in the street.

'See this bike? I don't have a use for it anymore,' he said. 'It might look fucked. But it's not.' Jack liked to swear when he spoke, for no particular reason, which annoyed my mother.

The bicycle was held together with rusted wire and old rope. I didn't want it but didn't have the courage to say so.

'Leave it here,' I said, 'on the verandah. I'll have to ask Mum when she gets in.'

While Mum didn't approve of Jack's foul language she told me I would have to show gratitude to him and accept the generous offer of the bike.

'I'm not riding that bike, Mum,' I told her.

'You'll accept the bike, and you'll ride it,' she ordered.

'I'm not doing it. I'll be laughed at.'

She wouldn't hear of it. 'All you need to do is ride the bike up and down the street now and then, so Jack can see that the bike has been put to use.'

The bike weighed a ton. Jack had attached a metal crate to the pack rack to help carry his workbag and bottles of beer. It added further weight to the machine that could well have been made of cast iron.

I did as my mother told me and rode the bike out on the street anytime I saw Jack out the front of his place, seated on a wooden chair and nursing a glass of beer. He would wave at me, I'd wave back, and he seemed happy enough. I had no intention of riding the bike any further than the end of the street until the morning I was about to mount it and my younger brother, Pat, who'd been watching me closely from the footpath, came and stood in front of the bike and took hold of the front wheel.

'What are you doing?' I said. 'Move. Or I'll ride over the top of you.'

'I want to come on the bike,' he said.

'I'm not going anywhere. Just to the bottom of the street and back.'

He refused to move. 'Take me on the bike. Please.'

Pat was a stubborn kid. When he got an idea in his head, he wouldn't shake it.

'I'll give you one ride, down to the corner and back. You got it? Just one.'

He nodded his head vigorously. Pat preferred animated gestures to speaking.

'Jump into the crate,' I ordered.

He looked anxiously at the crate. 'Is it safe?'

'I wouldn't think so. There couldn't be much to this bike that's safe. If you want a ride you'll have to take your life in your hands.'

Pat's slight body fitted easily into the crate. I pushed the bike onto the road, mounted it and began pedalling. It wobbled from side to side before steadying. We rode to the top end of the street, turned and headed downhill. I pedalled harder and the bike picked up speed. Pat wrapped his arms around me, pressed the side of his head into my back and squealed with fear and joy.

We raced down the hill and the bike crossed the street, picking up more speed as it went. I steered between a parked car and a fire hydrant and onto the empty allotment we used for making bonfires and playing marbles. I let the bike drop and slammed my shoulder into the dirt.

Pat flew through the air above me and hit the ground hard. He rolled over, spat dirt from his mouth and laughed. 'Can we do that again, Thom?'

I went to bed that night with a bruise on my chest and a graze on my shoulder. Pat had a lump on the side of his head but neither of us complained. However ridiculous the old bike looked, we'd enjoyed the ride.

The next day was Sunday. We got up early and quickly ate a breakfast of toast and tea. I went into the yard to collect the bike. 'Where are you going so early?' Mum asked.

'We're taking the bike out.'

'You mean the one you didn't want to be seen dead on?'

'Yep, that one.'

Out on the street I held the bike and Pat climbed into the metal crate. 'Where do you want to ride to?' I asked.

'You pick,' he said. 'I just want to go fast.'

We turned the corner and rode past the shops on the main street, most of which were closed for the day. A tram rushed by and the driver rang his bell and waved at us. Pat held on to me with one hand and waved to the driver with the other. I pedalled harder, trying to keep up with the tram but it soon got away from us.

We rode all over the suburb that morning – the main streets, side streets and laneways. We rode through the old gasworks that had closed down a year earlier, and on through the park where the old Chinese man from the Sun Moon cafe sat perfectly still under a tree each morning. When we rode back home, we were exhausted and happy. Pat didn't say a lot. He never did. But he couldn't stop smiling. We sat on the footpath sharing a milk bottle full of water.

'Hey, Thom,' Pat said, quietly.

'What?'

'Do you think that I could get a bike of my own and we could ride together?'

'Yeah. One day.'

'What day will that be?'

'I don't know. Just one day.'

Around the same time as Jack Garrett gifted us his ancient bicycle, our mother was deeply in love with the American film actor James Stewart. She'd stuck a colour poster of him on the wall of our kitchen and watched his films whenever she got the chance. Her favourite James Stewart movie was *It's a Wonderful Life*. Although she'd seen it many times and always knew what was coming, we could rely on her to bawl her eyes out near the end of the film when the bankrupt George Bailey – the Jimmy Stewart character – is helped out by his friends, people returning favours after his lifetime of good deeds. My own favourite Jimmy Stewart film was *The Stratton Story*, which I first watched on the couch under a blanket one weekday when I was off school with the measles. I liked it because the movie was about a baseball player, Monty Stratton, and baseball movies always have a happy ending, usually closing with a home run.

A couple of weeks before Pat's eighth birthday we caught a tram into the city to the Regent cinema to see a James Stewart double feature, *The Man Who Shot Liberty Valence* and *Harvey*. The Regent was a beautiful picture theatre. The foyer was lit with hundreds of bright globes; it had a marble staircase and statues of Roman gods lined the walls of the cinema. The Jimmy Stewart character in the Western is more or less a coward who is mistaken for a hero, who then becomes a bit of a hero anyway. In *Harvey* the Stewart character has an imaginary friend, a giant rabbit. My mother rarely laughed when we were kids, but she did that night watching *Harvey*. The film didn't make much sense to me and I was bored, but Pat loved it. He leaned forward in his chair, rested his chin on the empty seat in front and didn't take his eyes off the screen lighting up his face.

It was a warm night and, after leaving the cinema, we walked home past a toyshop at the top end of the city. It was a favourite window-shopping destination. Although we couldn't afford to buy the toys on display, it never stopped us from enjoying looking. That night, the window was lit for Christmas and the toy display was dominated by a shining red dragster bike with a metallic red seat, whitewall tyres, chromed mudguards, a sissy bar and streamers. It was such a magnificent bike. Pat stood in front of the window, his nose pressed to the glass, adoring the bike.

'Come on, you two, it's getting late,' Mum said. 'You have school in the morning.'

Pat wouldn't leave the window and Mum had to pull him away. He kept his thoughts to himself until we'd turned into our street. 'I could ride with you,' he whispered to me.

'What?'

'I could ride with you,' he repeated.

'You already do ride with me,' I said. 'In the crate.'

'I could ride the red bike with you if it was my own bike.'

Mum overheard our conversation and I saw the immediate look of disappointment on her face. The dragster was beyond our reach. She knew it and so did I. But not Pat. Once a thought like that got hold of him he wouldn't give up on it. Mum put her arm around him and held him close as we walked into the house. By the time we'd gone to bed he seemed to have forgotten about the bike. He was more interested in talking about the movie *Harvey*.

'Did you see the rabbit?' he said.

'What rabbit?'

'The one in the movie.'

'There was no rabbit. That fella, he was crazy. He made up the story about the rabbit.'

'Nup,' Pat said.

'What do you mean, *nup*?'

'The rabbit. He saw it and I saw it.'

'Sure.' I laughed. 'And what did it look like?'

'It was a rabbit with big ears. And it was white. I saw it.'

On the morning of his birthday Pat woke early, got out of his bed and hopped into mine. Half asleep, I felt his warm body pressed against me and his breath on the back of my neck. I'd almost returned to sleep when he began singing 'Birthday', The Beatles song.

'Sing with me,' he said.

We sang 'Birthday' a second time, followed by 'Yellow Submarine', which I'd once sung to win a talent quest at the Christmas party at the shoe factory where Mum worked. The prize was a model red sports car.

Pat lifted the beat of the song, slapping his hand against my back. When we hit the chorus, he screamed, 'We all live in a yellow submarine ... a yellow submarine ... a yellow submarine.'

The racket woke Mum in the next room and she got out of bed. She stood at our door wearing a dressing-gown over a nightie. Her hair was down. It was near-white in colour. She blamed the change of her hair on our long-absent father, who had caused her endless grief during their marriage.

'He could have turned Jack Johnson white,' she'd say, by way of explanation, although I had no idea at the time who Jack Johnson was. Her rich silver mane reached down the middle of her back. Pat poked his head out of the blanket.

She sat down, kissed him on both checks and said, 'Happy birthday, love. You get up and I'll make you a special breakfast.'

'Of what?' Pat asked.

'Of pancakes.'

I was first out of bed and saw the red dragster before Pat did. It looked even more spectacular, parked in our kitchen, than it had in the toyshop window. When Pat saw his present, he opened his mouth and circled the bike without saying a word. He reached out a hand and lightly touched the banana-shaped red seat, the chrome high-rise handlebars, and the blue and red streamers attached to the grips. His mouth curved up slightly and he closed his eyes.

'Do you like it?' Mum asked, as excited as I was. 'It's all yours.'

Pat touched the seat again and nodded his head. 'I love it.'

Mum noticed me also admiring the bike. While the pancakes sizzled on the stove, she whispered to me. 'You'll be next, Thom. For a new bike.'

I'd never had a new bike. I'd had no bike except for Jack Garrett's monster. I felt a little envious until later that morning, after we'd washed and dressed, and Mum took a photograph of Pat sitting on the bike. He hopped on the seat, leaned forward and wrapped his fists around the grips of the high-rise handlebars. His smile, at that moment, was the happiest I'd ever seen him – then or since. Pat's reaction to the bike pleased our mum so much she turned away so that he didn't see her tears and mistake them for sadness.

Later, in the street, Pat sat on the bike and put one hand on my shoulder. The other gripped the handlebar. Mum watched us from the footpath.

'Put your feet on the pedals,' I told him. 'We'll go uphill first. Slowly. I'll keep hold of the bike, so you don't fall off. Ready?'

'Yep,' he said, nervously.

He didn't look at all ready. His face was racked with anxiety.

I pushed the bike uphill and broke into a trot beside him. 'Pedal! Steer! Hold on!' I called, in no particular order.

Each time I released a hand from the bike, it wobbled from side to side and set off towards the gutter. After fifteen minutes of coaxing Pat to remain calm and ride steady I was sweating and breathing hard.

'I need a rest,' I said.

Pat hopped off, a look of defeat on his face.

Jack Garrett had been watching our cycling attempts from his verandah. He called us over to his house. 'I can fix your problem,' he said. 'Thommy, go and fetch my old bike and meet me back here.' He winked at Pat. 'We can't have your birthday fuck up on you.'

I retrieved my bike and when I returned, Jack was coming out of his house carrying a short metal bar with a metal coupling attached to each end. He carried a shifting spanner in his other hand. 'You two take a hold of one bike each,' he ordered. 'You, little fella,' he said to Pat, 'you stand that machine behind your brother's bike.'

Jack attached one of the couplings to the metal crate on my bike and the other to the neck of the handlebars of Pat's. He swore under his breath as he worked, for no particular reason that I could understand. When he'd tightened the couplings, he stood back and admired the dragster. 'So, this beautiful bicycle belongs to you?' he said to Pat.

'It's my birthday bike,' Pat said.

'Your mum, what a mighty woman she is. That's love from your mother, right there.'

Pat smiled at Jack.

'Right,' Jack said. 'Thommy, get on your bike.' He picked Pat up and sat him on the dragster. He then tapped the handlebars lightly with his spanner. 'Hold on here, but don't steer. Your brother will do that up front. But you do need to pedal. Get yourself used to it. Most of all, fucking hang on.'

Pat did as Jack instructed and gripped the handlebars.

'You,' Jack said to me. 'When you take off you'll have a bit of weight on your back. Like a fucking Melbourne Cup topweight. But you'll be right.' Mum had come out of our house and heard Jack swear. He shrugged his shoulders and smiled apologetically. 'Sorry, love.' Then he turned back to me. 'Go!' he ordered.

I started pedalling but the bike barely moved.

'More work on the pedals,' Jack yelled.

I gradually picked up speed and rode to the top of the street. When I turned to go downhill I could see Pat holding on and gritting his teeth. I didn't need to pedal downhill. The combined weight of both bikes and two bodies rapidly increased our speed.

As we passed Jack he barked more instructions. 'Brake easy, Thommy. Easy.'

Pat giggled, obviously unaware of the looming danger. I hit the brake, released and hit it again, and managed to stop the bike without crossing the street and most likely crashing.

'How good was that?' I said to Pat.

'The best.'

Jack waddled over to us. He put a hand on Pat's head and ruffled his curls. 'You do this for some time, little fella, then you come see me to take this bar off. You'll ride as good as anyone.'

We spent the next week riding around the streets with Pat's dragster attached to the back of my bike like a caboose on a train. It was the school holidays. We covered every street in the neighbourhood on our bikes, leaving the house after breakfast and riding all morning. We came back at lunchtime for a sandwich and a cup of tea and took off again. At the end of the week it was time for Pat to ride on his own. Jack removed the bar joining the bikes.

Pat hopped onto the seat of the dragster.

'I reckon you're ready,' I assured him. 'Pedal and steer is all you need to do.'

'I don't know,' he whispered. He didn't want Jack to hear that he was uneasy about riding alone.

'You can do it,' I said. 'I'm going to count down from three and you're going to ride. Three, two, one, go!'

Pat slammed his foot on the pedal. The bike didn't wobble and he rode to the top of the street, turned and came back downhill. His head of curls lifted in the breeze and Pat's face beamed. Riding by Jack and me, he rang the bell on the bike.

By the second week of the summer holidays we were riding side by side. In the afternoons we'd ride to the Exhibition Gardens for a swim. A bowl-shaped concrete pan had been built next to the children's playground and in summer, when the day was warm, a council worker arrived at the bowl early in the morning and turned on the water hydrants surrounding it. The bowl quickly filled and by lunchtime it was crowded with screaming kids. The water was shallow, only elbow deep, which suited Pat, who couldn't really swim. A paddle at the bowl was also free.

Welfare workers would turn up some days and give every kid a free icy pole. Mum warned us not to take one, 'Next thing you know they'll have you away.' We ignored her orders and took the icy poles anyway. I told Pat not to say a word when he was handed a sweet and not to answer any questions, which was never difficult for Pat to do. Once we'd been handed an icy pole each, we'd ride off on our bikes, to be certain that we were safe.

One afternoon, riding home from the gardens, I noticed a reflection on the bitumen pathway and hit the brake on my bike. 'Wait!' I called out to Pat who'd ridden on. I'd found a coin and showed it to him.

'Who does it belong to?' he asked.

'Us,' I said. 'It's ours.'

'But it was on the ground.'

'Which means that it's ours. But just in case, we'd better spend it before someone claims it.'

We rode to a nearby petrol station. The cafe next door to the station sold hamburgers and cold drinks. A group of kids were rollerskating around the petrol bowsers. We rested our bikes against one of the bowsers and went inside the cafe. Meat and onions sizzled on the hotplate.

'What do you want?' I asked Pat. 'We have enough money for chips and a milkshake each. Or one hamburger between us and two milkshakes.'

'You pick,' he said.

I ordered a hamburger and two chocolate milkshakes and we sat at a booth and waited. When it arrived, I broke the hamburger in half and watched Pat as he ate, slowly chewing each mouthful as if it was his last meal. We downed the milkshakes and left the cafe.

Pat's red dragster was missing.

'The bike!' I screamed. I grabbed hold of one of the rollerskating kids. 'Where's my brother's bike?'

He tried to break free. 'Fuck off. I don't know.'

I shook him. 'Where's his dragster? We left my brother's bike out here.'

One of the other skaters pointed to a high-rise estate across the street. 'Some boys from the flats took it,' he said. He was short and squat, with so many freckles on his face they bled into one dark birthmark.

'What boys?'

'From the estate. I don't know who they are. They came here on their own bikes while you were inside and took your bike with them.'

'What's their names?' I asked.

'I can't say that. They'll kill me.'

'How many of them are there?'

'Maybe four.' He shrugged. 'Or maybe five or six.'

Pat stood close to the doorway of the cafe. He was about to cry. 'Your bike's been knocked off,' I said. 'We have to get it back.'

'Not if it's trouble, Thom. I don't want trouble.'

'Don't be a coward, Pat. Get in the fucking crate.'

I picked him up, dumped him in the metal crate and rode as hard as I could across the street to the high-rise, a no-go area for any kid who didn't live there. I turned into the estate and saw the dragster straightaway. A kid around my age was riding it on one wheel, mono-style. A gang of boys sat on the grass watching him. I jumped off my bike, forgetting that Pat was in the crate. I let it drop to the ground and he fell out, onto the grass.

The kid on the bike rode past me like he didn't care at all that he was a bicycle thief. As he turned and rode back in my direction I leaped in front of him and grabbed the handlebars. He jumped off and grabbed hold of the seat, starting a tug of war over the bike.

'You stole this from my brother,' I said. 'Let fucking go of it.'

'Get fucked,' he yelled. 'I stole nothing.'

The other boys created a circle around us. I pulled as hard as I could on the bike and freed it. The circle closed in on me. 'This is my brother's bike,' I said. 'I'm taking it home.'

A car turned into the estate and screeched to a halt alongside us. Two older teenage boys got out. One of them had a tattoo, a crucifix on the back of one arm, a backyard job. He said to the kid I'd wrestled the bike from, 'What's going on?'

'We found this bike at the servo and he just comes here and says it belongs to him. But it doesn't.'

'What the fuck are you doing here?' the older boy said to me.

I held the dragster by the handlebars and seat. I was afraid but tried not to show it. 'This bike belongs to my little brother. My mum bought it for his birthday and these kids stole it from us. I'm not leaving here without it.'

'And what makes you think you'd get away with that?'

'Because my mum saved up and bought it for him. It cost her a lot of money. I'm taking the bike with me.'

He jabbed me in the chest. 'And how much of a fight would you put up to keep it?'

I thought about James Stewart in *The Man Who Shot Liberty Valance* and a scene in the film where he has to make a choice if he's going to remain a coward or learn to be brave.

'I'd fight as hard as I could,' I said.

'My little brother said he found the bike, and that it's his now.'

'I fucking did find it,' the young brother added.

Pat broke through the circle, stood in front of the older boy, who towered over him, and rested a hand on the bike seat. 'This bike belongs to me.'

'Boo!' the older boy roared. Pat cowered and the circle of boys laughed at him. The older boy turned to the driver of the car. 'What do you reckon?'

His mate shrugged his shoulders.

'You take the bike and fuck off,' he said to me. 'And don't come back. This is our place. You step foot on the estate again, I'll kick a hole in you.'

I wheeled the dragster out of the circle and helped Pat mount the bike. 'Ride home,' I whispered. 'And don't stop until you get there.'

'What about you?' he asked, staring over at the gang of boys.

'I'll be behind you. But don't you stop or look back. Ride as fast as you can.'

I waited until Pat had ridden safely away and collected my bike from the ground.

The older boy blocked my path. 'Maybe you need a belting anyway,' he said, 'to be sure you get the message?'

'I came for my brother's bike. That's all. I won't be coming back here.'

'Fuck off, then,' he said, 'before I change my mind.'

The younger boy who'd stolen Pat's bike was angry. 'I found the bike at the servo. And he took it back. He has to pay for it.'

'Shut up!' the older boy said, slapping the younger kid on the side of the head. 'Next time you thieve something, see if you can do it without being caught.'

Pat was waiting for me on a corner two streets away. We rode home and didn't say a word about what had happened. If Mum found out we'd been in any sort of trouble, she'd keep us inside for the rest of the holidays.

In bed that night, after the light had been turned off, Pat called out to me in the darkness.

'Thom.'

'Yep.'

'We were lucky today, to find the bike after we lost it.'

We were lucky we hadn't been beaten up and had found the bike. 'Yeah. We were lucky, but we didn't lose the dragster, Pat. The bike was stolen from us.'

'Thom.'

'Go to sleep, Pat.'

'Thom. I love you.'

The following day Mum left me a list of shopping to pick up at the supermarket. Pat didn't want to help and stayed at home on the couch watching *Bonanza*. I told him that he could ride his dragster if he wanted to but wasn't to leave the street.

When I came home an hour later, with the trolley full of shopping, Pat was sitting on the footpath outside the house with his head buried between his legs. Hearing the squeaking wheels of the trolley, he looked up at me. His cheeks were flushed and his eye was swollen. The red dragster lay on the footpath next to him. It looked like a giant broken bird. The seat had been reversed, the spokes on both wheels were bent and the streamers were missing. I picked the bicycle up. The frame was bent out of shape.

'What happened?' I shouted. 'Did you have an accident?'

Pat wiped his face. 'Those boys from yesterday, they came here when you were at the market. They took the bike and threw it in the air. And then they jumped on it and broke it.'

'Did they touch you?'

'Nup.' He buried his face in his hands and cried. 'They laughed at me. One of them said I was spastic.'

I sat down next to him on the footpath and put my arm around him until he stopped crying. We knocked on Jack Garrett's door and showed him the damage to the bike and told him what had happened. He picked the bike up and uttered, 'Cunts, cunts, cunts,' as he inspected it.

'I can't fix this,' he said. 'The frame is fucked. You need to take it down to the scrapyard behind The Valley hotel. You need to see a fella called Dominic. Blackfella. He owns the yard. You tell him Jack Garrett sent you. If he can't straighten the frame, no-one can.'

We dragged the bike to the scrapyard, where we found Jack's mate, Dominic. He took one look at the bike and said, 'I reckon I would have more chance of salvaging the *Titanic* than I do this bicycle. It's fucked. I mean really fucked.'

'That's what Jack reckoned,' I said.

'Well, old Jack's right. How'd the bike get this way? It looks like it's taken a terrible beating.'

I told him about the boys from the estate coming around to our street and wrecking the bike.

'Cunts!'

'Yep. Jack said that too.'

Dominic ruffled Pat's curls. 'I'm really sorry for you. The little cunts,' he repeated. He then offered us ten dollars for the bike. 'Not that it's worth that much,' he added. 'But it's the only compensation you're going to get.' Then he looked purposely at me and added, 'Unless you can give them boys that did this a dishful of punishment. That's what they fucking need. A decent hiding.'

I handed the money to Pat. 'I want you to go home and

give this money to Mum. You need to tell her the truth about what happened to the bike. There's no getting out of this with a story.'

'What about you? What are you going to do?'

'I'm going to be doing nothing you need to know about.'

He tugged nervously at a curl of his hair. 'But I want to come with you.'

'No, you don't, Pat. You get home and wait inside. Put the TV on and watch cartoons until Mum gets home from work.'

When I got home later that day, in darkness, Mum was leaning on the verandah rail. She'd been waiting for me. My condition didn't seem to surprise her at all. She inspected my bloodied shirt, the three missing buttons and torn pocket. Dry blood was caked under my nose and my left eye had already blackened. She stood back and looked me up and down. Another kid might have got a hug or a kiss from his mother. Not me. Mum and me, we were never affectionate with each other. I'd always known that she saved her love for Pat, and I didn't really mind. I could take care of myself.

'Those bastards,' she said, 'wrecking his bike. Why'd you go back there, Thom? What were you hoping for?'

I smiled at her. 'A black eye.'

'Well, you've got a beauty. Come in and wash and eat.'

The following morning Jack Garrett congratulated me. 'Anyone who steals another person's bike is a low fucking dog,' he said. We were standing in the middle of the street. Pat had once more been relegated to the metal crate of Jack's old contraption.

'You did well for yourself, Thommy boy. There's nothing wrong with losing. It's how you lose, and you did so with bravery. They won't forget you, and they'll never steal from you again. You've got them on the fucking run.'

I didn't know that Jack was right but I appreciated what he said.

He shook his head and rested an arm on Pat's shoulder. 'Your big brother here, you know he'll always be there for you? I wish I'd had a brother looking after me when I was coming up on the street. Your Thommy, he's a guardian angel at your back.'

'I know,' Pat said. He looked at me. 'I really do.'

'Around this way,' Jack continued, 'it used to be: *Thou Shalt Not Steal Another's Bicycle.* It was the first commandment of the streets. Good words.' He sighed. 'They're worth fuck-all these days.'

PROBATE

S TAN DIDN'T LOOK GOOD. From the window, I could see him
in the garden. Hunched forward, sucking on a cigarette,
mistaking it for a sign of life, he was mumbling to himself.
I signed the visitors' book, spoke to the house manager and
stood watching him. Thoughts of turning around and leaving
the nursing home without speaking to him were hard to
shake off.

Stan had always been one for nostalgia. Right now, I thought,
he was most likely reminiscing about his days as a street runner,
scammer and budding career criminal. He also loved to tell
stories about his life as an armed robber. The big hauls he'd
pulled, the petrified bank tellers he'd terrorised, or the values
of a side-by-side double-barrel shotgun as opposed to an over-
and-under. If memory is selective, Stan's was tellingly so. He
neglected the tales of his attacks on women and family, and the
occasional whisper in a detective's ear, to ensure he held onto
the keys to the city.

I knocked on the glass sliding door. Stan twitched nervously, possibly thinking an old adversary had come to pay him an unwelcome visit. I opened the door and stepped into the garden.

Close up, he looked frail. Cheeks sunken, he'd obviously dropped weight. The jagged scar on his right cheek had changed colour. Blood pink, it looked like a recent war wound, rather than a thirty-year-old battle scar. If Stan had lifted his shirt his torso would display a life of violence, including a near-death experience. More scars, bullet wounds and physical deterioration.

'You came?' he said, without looking at me. 'Wasn't sure you'd turn up.'

'The message said it was urgent.'

'Really?' He seemed genuinely puzzled. 'All I said was to ask if you could come. There was no urgency.'

Stan had always been a man of blunt words, and I'd never enjoyed talking to him. I didn't see any need for a cosy chat now. 'So, what do you want? You must have asked me here for something.'

'I'm dying,' he said. 'Soon.'

The words registered but had no impact on me. 'I guess it is urgent then. What have you got?'

'Doesn't matter what the fuck it is,' he said. 'It's the end.'

He spoke with no more interest in his death than I had. He wouldn't fear death, I was certain of that.

What puzzled me was why he'd felt the need to ask me to the nursing home to tell me this. Stan had never been one to travel lightly. Whatever the reason I was standing in the garden with him, it would come with baggage.

'You wanna sit?' he asked.

Being physically close to Stan had always resulted in discomfort. 'I'm good,' I replied.

'The last visit by the doc here, he said maybe a month or two, probably less.' He paused. I wondered if he was waiting for a comment from me. Or even a show of sympathy, so out of character, I couldn't imagine it. 'The next day some young prick of a lawyer come by. Public Advocate office. Says I need to get my affairs in order. Starting with a discussion about a funeral.'

If Stan was about to ask me to preside over his coffin, he had to be senile. He knew how I felt about him, and that nothing would change with his demise. 'Funeral?' I questioned.

'Well, not as such,' he said. 'There'd be no-one there to cry over me. Maybe one or two to spit on the coffin, at best. No, I said the university could have me, you know, cut me up. He said that's not on. They have an oversupply. Fuck me.' He coughed furiously and his battered face turned to purple. 'So, I need you to help.'

I had no intention of looking after Stan's affairs. 'Why me?'

'Because there's no-one fucking else,' he roared, briefly introducing the fearful menace of old. 'All you need to do is be certain these fuckwits that run this place follow my instructions. Simple.'

'And what are they?'

'After I'm dead, I've nominated a funeral mob. They pick me up, no coffin, nothing, then they burn me, give the ashes to you and you get rid of them however you want.'

'Can't they – the funeral home – get rid of you, your ashes? Why do you need me?'

'I tried that.' Stan appeared as frustrated as I was. 'They don't like that. It gets complicated. They won't dispose of me without tracking down living relatives, they said. It's messy. The fella said I could be stuck sitting on a shelf for years. Fuck that.' He looked at me. His eyes almost softened. 'It's not much. All you need to do is pick up the ashes. Throw them in a bin as soon as you leave the joint, if you like. Or flush me down the toilet. I don't give a fuck.'

I sensed that he did give a fuck. 'If you don't care either way, Stan, why don't you just sit on that shelf? You might have company.'

He hesitated before answering and, when he did, he spoke in a whisper. 'Because I don't want them thinking no-one, not a soul, wanted me.'

Fuck, I thought. Even the homicidal Stanley Rook could be beaten by self-pity.

'Will you do it?' he asked.

While I wasn't keen to carry out his orders, there seemed no harm in telling him I'd agree to his wishes. If I changed my mind, Stan would never know. No harm done. 'Okay. I'll do it. So, what would you prefer: the bin or the toilet bowl?'

'I don't care. Whatever is easiest for you. I reckon you'd like to piss on my remains. Do that if you like.'

'There would be a few others interested in that.' I smiled. 'Maybe I could arrange a wake and we'll all piss on you.'

'Whatever you want,' he said. 'It will be your party, not mine.'

A nursing sister appeared at the doorway. 'You will need to come in soon, Mr Rook. The wind has picked up. We don't want you catching a cold.'

'I've got throat cancer,' he barked at her. 'What do I care if I end up with a cold. Fuck off.'

'I see you're still polite with the ladies,' I said.

He looked down at the hands he'd done so much damage with. 'How's your mother?' he asked. 'Is she still alive?'

I didn't want to get into a conversation with Stan about my mother. 'She's good.'

'Did she ever remarry?'

'Hey, Stan, drop it. She wouldn't want me talking to you about her. She doesn't even know I'm here.'

'Will you tell her?'

'That I visited you? No.'

'I mean, will you tell her after I'm gone, that I've died?'

'Of course, I'll tell her. She might be old, Stan, but she's entitled to some joy in her life.'

Stan laughed. 'I like that. She's entitled to a laugh. I was a cunt of a husband and a father.'

I wasn't about to disagree with him and said nothing.

He slowly got to his feet. 'Look at you,' he said.

'What's that mean?'

He placed a hand on my shoulder. I froze. 'When you were a kid, you were soft. Too soft. I was ashamed of you. Do you know that?'

'Oh, I know it. I still have the scars to show for your shame.' My voice rose. 'Would you like to see them, Stan?'

He patted my shoulder several times. 'Take it easy. I was going to say, you've changed. You have presence now, son. Back in the day, running with me, you'd have made a decent robber. You'd have needed training, of course. You'd put the fear into people.'

Fear. It was all that Stan knew. And he was good at it. One of the best. But Stan was a one-trick pony. He knew no other skill in life, which was why he was sitting in a garden, in a nursing home, soon to die alone.

'You better go,' he said. 'We have dinner here at five and then it's off to our rooms. It's fucking worse in here than being in the nick. Fuck, I done H Division in the old days, it's nothing on this place. Get going.'

I looked at Stan for the final time. Once, one of his brothers, Des, had come snooping around our place when Stan was away doing three years. Mum said that Stan would have sent Des to check up on her, to make sure she didn't have a man around the house.

Des had lifted my chin and said, 'You're the spitting image of your father.' My mother looked at Des with disgust and I dropped my head in shame.

'I'll see you then, Stan,' I said.

'No, you won't. Never again.'

Three weeks later, Stan was dead. I was walking near the sea when my phone rang. The nursing sister asked if I'd like to visit the home and spend time with my father's body before he was collected by the funeral home responsible for the cremation.

'I'm sure that you would enjoy some contemplative time and perhaps prayer with your father,' she offered.

'No, I don't need to do that. Thank you. I've done my contemplation.'

I stopped for a moment, closed my eyes and listened to the waves rolling in and sliding out; a feat of predictability and calmness I envied. I put the phone away and continued my walk.

The following week a parcel arrived in the mail. It was half the size of a house brick and weighed more than I would have expected. I unwrapped the parcel. Inside was a sealed box, secured with gaffer tape. A label on the box read: *Stanley James Rook – Remains*. An accompanying letter explained that the ashes of my father were now mine, and that if I wished to dispose of them I needed to do so *responsibly*, adding that some municipalities do not permit the *disposal of human remains within their administrative jurisdiction*.

I sat the box on the kitchen bench and left it there for the afternoon and into the evening while I cooked my dinner. I went to bed that night without touching the box again.

In the morning, it was exactly where I'd left it – irrationally I'd hoped that it might simply vanish, relieving me of any responsibility.

In a phone call I had let my mother know that Stan was dead. She said very little and expressed neither joy nor sadness. For several weeks, I moved my father around the house – to the mantel in the lounge, to a cupboard drawer, to the balcony next to a potted fern.

When my mother came for lunch about a month later, Stan's ashes were sitting on a bookshelf. She noticed the box as soon as she came into the house. She picked up the box and shook it.

'He rattles,' she said, and put him back down. 'What are you going to do? Get an urn, I suppose?'

That wasn't my intention. 'No, Mum, I'm going to get rid of the ashes. I just haven't got around to doing it.'

'Get rid of them?' She was visibly shocked.

'Yeah. I talked about it with him. He said he didn't care what happened.'

'You spoke to him? Your father?'

I told her about my visit to the nursing home in the weeks before his death. If she was angry at all, it didn't show.

'You can't do that,' she said.

'I can't what?'

'Get rid of your father's ashes. Dispose of him.'

I couldn't believe what she'd said. 'Why can't I?'

'Because he's your father. Blood. It would be wrong to do so.'

I picked up the box and offered it to her. 'You can have him, if you like.'

'It's not for me to have him. But you need to. Like I said. Blood. You get rid of him now, there'll be a day when you regret it.'

'I don't think so, Mum.'

'Think what you like. I'm your mother and I know.'

She left soon after lunch, mildly unhappy with me. I sat on the couch and looked across the room at Stan, annoyed that he'd come back into our lives, even in death. I vowed that the next morning I would get rid of him.

When my mother visited next, she headed straight for the bookshelf, picked up the box and shook it. She seemed pleased to again hear the rattle of Stan's remains.

We sat and began quietly eating lunch. She bit into a ham and pickle sandwich on wholemeal bread. Her favourite. I glanced across the room, spotting the opened packet of kitty litter left sitting on the bottom shelf of the bookcase.

STARMAN

I FELL IN LOVE WITH Marnie Smith the day her father bought a European stereo system. It had an unpronounceable name and the sweetest sound I'd ever heard. At the time, I was walking upstairs to our flat on the third floor and passed Marnie's open door. The landing outside her flat was being torn to shreds by David Bowie's 'Suffragette City'. I stopped and listened to the frantic opening bars. The music entered both ears, spun around my head, headed south and shook my body. Marnie and I had gone to primary school together, but went our separate ways before our first year in high school. While I attended the local public school, Marnie was sent off to a private school where the students climbed trees and told teachers to 'fuck off' at will.

Marnie came to the door, wearing a pair of Levi's and a Harlem Globetrotters singlet. She wore her dark hair short, was often mistaken for a boy and was the best basketball player on the estate, from street games to the local church league.

'Hey, Dylan,' she said.

'Heya, Marnie. That's Bowie.'

'Yeah, Bowie,' she drawled. 'The new album. Have you heard it?'

'Just a couple of tracks on *The Album Hour,* on our three-in-one. It sounds nothing like this.'

'I'm sure it doesn't.' She smiled and nodded her head. Although we were both fifteen at the time, Marnie looked older than me. 'Hey, Dylan,' she repeated. 'Would you like to listen to the whole album?'

I felt my cheeks heat as I blushed. 'Sure. When?'

'On the weekend. You can come by on Saturday afternoon, if you like. Are you free on Saturday?'

I had no idea if I was free or not, but was certain I'd make myself available. 'Saturday would be good. Yeah.'

She came out onto the landing and leaned against the stairway bannister. 'You'll have to bring something to the table though. An entry fee.'

'Like what?'

'Like one of your own albums that we can listen to together. The best you've got. One that I don't have, hopefully. What's your favourite record? It can't be any of the old stuff that your mum and dad buy from the World Record Club. If I have to listen to one more Tom Jones song, I'll die. He grows his hair long and gets some sideburns and he thinks he's cool.' She leaped over the bannister onto the stairs. 'What have you got that might impress me, Dylan?'

'What about *Electric Warrior,* T. Rex.'

'Yeah,' she said. 'Well done, Dylan. That just might get you all the way with Bang & Olufsen.'

'Who are they?' I asked.

'Oh, don't you worry.' She leaned forward and flicked a lock of hair from my shoulder. 'That's why you wear your hair long, isn't it? Marc Bolan?'

'What about him?'

'You want to be Marc Bolan. It makes perfect sense. The long hair and your red shirt. No-one wears a red shirt around here. Not a boy, at least. I like that about you, Dylan. You might just be daring.'

Of course, I wanted to be Marc Bolan, but it wasn't something I'd admit outside my bedroom, in front of the mirror playing air guitar. I also wanted to be daring.

'What's your favourite track on the album?' she asked.

I didn't hesitate. '"Jeepster".'

'Of course. I know why you boys love that song.'

'Why?' I asked

'It's the last line, *I'm gonna suck you.* That's the line you all love to sing, real loud. Isn't it? *I'm gonna suck you.*'

Marnie was right. 'No. It's not that line. Not for me, anyway.'

'Really?' She seemed genuinely surprised. 'What's your favourite line then?'

'It's, *Girl, I'm just a jeepster for your love.*'

'Oh. Nice one, Dylan. That is some line. You'll go far with that line.'

Mrs Jensen, from the top floor, interrupted our conversation as she lugged the family shopping upstairs in four string bags. 'That racket is a bit loud,' she complained.

'If you like I can turn it up for you, Mrs Jensen,' Marnie offered.

Mrs Jensen grunted under her breath and continued climbing.

'What about you, Marnie?' I asked.

'What do you mean?' she said.

'Who do you want to be, other than yourself?'

'Oh. Different people. It depends on how I feel and what day it is. We can wait and see on Saturday. Come at two o'clock.'

'Two?'

'Yeah. My mum and dad will be out. They have these other hippie friends, just like them, who have an olive farm in the countryside. Do you know that olives actually grow on trees? I didn't know that.'

I didn't know it either. The closest I'd come to an olive was in a jar at the Italian delicatessen at the shops, but I'd never eaten one.

'They drive to the country and they pick olives and drink wine with their friends. Maybe they wife-swap too. I'm not sure. They won't be home until late. So, two o'clock. Do you think that maybe you should write it down, Dylan?'

I was sure there was no need to write the time and place down. 'I'll be here.'

I was too excited to go home. I bypassed our place and headed for the rooftop. A couple of mums were sitting outside the laundry, enjoying a smoke while they waited for the washing to dry. I could see Peter Kidd lying on top of the laundry wearing only his jeans. A T-shirt covered his face. I walked behind the laundry and climbed the makeshift ladder onto the roof.

'Kidd. What are you doing?'

He took the T-shirt away from his face and sat up. Kidd, as everyone called him, was sporting the worst haircut I'd ever seen. The top of his head had been shaven and straps of long hair reached down the middle of his naked back.

'Jesus, Kidd. Who got to your hair? Have you had nits or something?'

He ran a hand across his close-cropped skull. 'Fuck off. I paid good money for this, Dylan. It's a sharpie cut.'

'You paid for it? At the blind school?'

Kidd rolled onto his stomach and looked over the ledge of the roof, to the bare ground five storeys below us. 'Yeah, I paid for it. And it's a good haircut.'

'But you're not a skinhead, Kidd. No-one is around here. That head could get you a kicking in this neighbourhood.'

'Maybe so. But not in Preston. They like this haircut out in Preston.' He spat over the ledge. We watched as the gorby careered to the ground, just missing the gardener's head. 'They love it. Everybody has one.'

'But you don't live in Preston, Kidd. We're a long way from Preston here.'

'I know,' he said, grinning.

'I get it,' I said. 'You've done this for a girl. A Preston girl.'

'That's right. You're a genius, Dylan.'

'Where'd you meet her?'

'At the alley.' Kidd worked at the Mutual Bowl in the city, racking pins. 'She was with a gang of girls. I let them have a few free games and we got talking.'

'You butchered your hair because a girl from Preston spoke to you? That's sacrifice.'

'It wasn't just the talk. Afterwards we went for a walk in the gardens on St Kilda Road.'

'Now, that's a different matter,' I said, and whistled. 'A walk in the gardens. I'd shave my head bald for a walk in the gardens with a girl.'

'It gets better. Last week, she invited me to her place for Sunday roast. With the family. We had chicken.'

'Sunday roast with the in-laws. This is getting serious, Kidd.' I laughed. 'Now I understand why you did it, shaved your head. What's she like, this Preston girl?'

He buried his face in his hands. 'Beautiful, Dylan. She is beautiful.'

'Does she have a haircut the same as this one?'

'Yep. Just the same,' he said.

'Now I really get it. And what music does she listen to?'

'Slade. Sharps and skins love Slade.'

Slade weren't a bad band, although I'd never bother to buy one of their records. 'Can you ask her something on my behalf?'

'Sure. What is it?'

'Why do sharpies and skinheads love Slade when the lead singer, Noddy Holder, has more hair on his head than Cousin Itt? I don't get that.'

He spat over the ledge again. The gorby landed on the top of the gardener's balding head. By the time he'd looked up we'd retreated.

'Maybe they're being ironic?' Kidd said.

'I don't think so. Not in Preston. They go to tech out that way. Never get past woodwork.' I nudged him in the ribs. 'I want to tell you about a girl.'

'Go on,' he said, lazily, preoccupied by thoughts of a beautiful girl from Preston.

'Marnie Smith,' I said.

'What about her?'

'I just saw her on the landing. She has a stereo system. A proper one.'

'Is that it? Congratulations, Dylan.'

'We were just talking, and then she invited me over on Saturday to listen to music with her. She made a point of telling me that her parents will be out. All I have to do is bring one of my own records. She said we can share, Kidd. *Share.*'

'And what are you taking with you, to share?'

'*Electric Warrior.*'

'A fine choice, Dylan. I used to listen to Marc Bolan before I became a sharpie.' He turned onto his back and covered his face with his T-shirt again. 'You know, they say that she's different?'

'Who?'

'Marnie. The girl you were just talking about. You've forgotten her already.'

'Different? In what way?' I asked.

'Can't say. She just is. Maybe it's that weird school she goes to. They don't have uniforms there. Anything's possible once you get rid of a school uniform. You better watch yourself with her.'

'Don't worry about me. You watch yourself out in Preston. They could see past that haircut and kill you.'

When I told my older sister, Valerie, I was going to Marnie Smith's place on Saturday to listen to music, she shouted the news out the window to Lisa Love, her best friend, who lived in the block across the way.

Later in the afternoon, they sat me in Valerie's bedroom and interrogated me.

'What are you going to wear?' Lisa asked.

'I'm not sure,' I said. 'I haven't thought about it.'

'Well, we need you to think now,' Valerie said. 'The wrong fashion choice can make the difference between love and a broken heart.'

'Well,' I said. 'I think I'll wear my Dee Cee jeans.'

'I like that,' Lisa said. 'Not many wear Dee Cee around here. They're imported. That will impress her more than a pair of 501s. I like that. And a top?'

'Probably one of my Miller shirts, with the pearl buttons.'

Valerie wasn't impressed. 'I don't think so, Dylan. That's a bit too Creedence Clearwater for me. I don't see Marnie Smith going for that. She's more your Doors type of woman. Leather.'

'What if I wear the shirt with the gold thread through it?'

'That might work,' Lisa offered. 'A sort of glam-rock cowboy. She might go for that?'

'Nup,' Valerie said. 'That will never work.' She clicked her fingers. 'Dylan, take your T-shirt off.'

I didn't want to take my top off in front of Lisa Love. 'Why?' I asked.

'Because, I said. You want to stay a virgin all your life?'

'Leave him be,' Lisa said. 'He's only fifteen.'

'You weren't a virgin at fifteen,' Valerie said. 'I don't want my brother bullied. His time has come to shed and spread.'

I stood up and pulled my T-shirt over my head.

'Hey, little man, not a bad body for your age,' Lisa said. 'If Marnie Smith knocks you back, come over to my place. My mum will be on night shift and my dad will be passed out pissed on the couch.'

'Stop teasing him,' Valerie said. 'This is serious.' She pulled a long-sleeved ribbed top from her drawer. Black with lime and orange stripes across the front. 'Put this on.'

I put the jumper on. It was a little tight and hugged my body. Lisa wolf-whistled and slapped me on the arse. 'Nice work, Valerie. Your little brother looks seriously rootable in that.'

Valerie ignored the comment. 'Dylan. Look in the mirror. Do you like it?'

I stood in front of the mirror and admired the jumper. I did like it. 'Yeah. You think I should wear this?'

'We do,' Lisa said. 'Make sure you wash your hair on Friday night and clean your teeth. Give me a look at your fingernails.'

I showed my hands. My fingernails were clean.

'That's good,' Lisa said. 'I went out with Rojo, that fella from the bottle yard. We were just about to slip into the back seat of his car and I saw all this dirt under his fingernails. That was it for me. I left him and walked home.'

'You never told me you went out with Rojo,' Valerie said.

'Because I didn't go out with him. I just told you. I gave him the flick.'

Valerie raked her fingers through my curls. 'Okay, Dylan. When you kiss for the first few times, no experimentation. Play safe. No tongue.'

'Definitely no tongue,' Lisa added. 'If a boy doesn't know how to tongue-kiss proper, and most don't, it feels like you have someone shoving a cold piece of lamb's fry in your mouth. Awful.'

Valerie rested her hands on my shoulders. 'Now, Dylan, how will you answer the big question? It will come up, you can be sure of that. It always does. You need to give the right answer.'

'What's the question?' I asked.

'Are you a virgin?' Lisa laughed.

'Shut up,' Valerie said. 'This is serious, Lisa. I want my little brother to come home with a smile on his face. The question,' she said to me, 'is this: The Rolling Stones or The Beatles?'

'Sorry?' I asked.

'Focus, Dylan. Focus. At some point, this girl, Marnie, is going to ask if you prefer The Beatles or The Rolling Stones. And the answer you give will matter. It could be the difference between you-know-what and nothing.'

'Now,' Lisa said, 'if she likes poetry types, you'd go for The Beatles. If she's after a wild ride, it has to be The Stones.'

'She's only fifteen,' I pleaded. 'And I'm only fifteen.'

'I was after a ride at fifteen,' Lisa offered. 'But I couldn't get one. The trouble with fifteen-year-old boys is they're so timid. Backward. I'm worried that you might be a timid one, Dylan.'

'Lisa, please shut up,' Valerie said. 'What's your answer, Dylan?'

'I don't know,' I said. 'I like The Beatles and The Stones. Do I have to pick?'

'You do have to pick,' Valerie said. 'If I was out with a date, or *in*, and a fella gave me that answer, I'd get rid of him. Fence sitter.'

The whole Beatles vs Stones question made no sense to me. None of their advice did. I was going to Marnie Smith's house to play records. 'Why would you do that,' I asked Valerie, 'if he liked The Beatles and The Rolling Stones as much as each other?'

'Because,' Lisa said, 'that's the sign of a man who can't make a decision, because he doesn't know what he wants. You best think of something more than *I like them both*, Dylan. That is not an answer.'

The following Saturday I walked down one flight of stairs at five to two in the afternoon with *Electric Warrior* tucked under one arm.

Marnie opened her front door wearing a pair of cut-off faded Levi's, Indian toe-sandals and a Miller shirt, red-chequered, pearl buttons. 'Wow, Dylan, that top is really something. And you've washed your hair. I can tell by the way it sits.'

'And I cleaned my teeth,' I said, before realising it was possibly a stupid comment.

'Good boy,' she said. 'Hygiene. Wow. Do you like my shirt? This is the first time I've worn it.'

'Yeah,' I said. 'It's sort of Creedence Clearwater Revival.'

'It is. Very CCR.'

'You look like a cowgirl,' I said.

Marnie was having none of it. 'No, Dylan. I'm a cowboy.'

She closed the front door and offered me a glass of lemonade. 'Do you want ice?' she asked.

'No. I'm fine.'

The flat was decorated with what looked like expensive furniture and rugs. Pictures lined the walls, not photographs, but *art*, I guessed. I wondered if Marnie's parents fenced stolen goods.

'Do you like our place?' she said.

'Yeah. It looks nice.'

'Okay. You come and sit with me.'

'Do you want the album?' I asked. 'To play it?'

'That can wait. Let's talk first.' She guided me to a couch in the lounge room. 'Hey, Dylan, who knows you're here? I'm only asking in case I need to tie you up.' She scrunched her nose up like a cat and smiled.

'Well,' I said. 'My older sister, Valerie, her friend, Lisa, and Peter Kidd.'

'Peter Kidd! Why did you tell him? I've never liked Peter Kidd.'

'I only told him because he was up on the roof and was telling me about some beautiful girl from Preston that he's in love with. So I told him about you.'

'Preston?'

'Yeah. It's hard to believe.'

'And what did you tell him about me?'

'That you had a brilliant stereo system,' I said.

'And what else?'

'That's it, really. And that you knew a lot of stuff about music.'

'And what did Peter Kidd say? Anything about me?'

I hesitated.

'Go on,' she demanded. 'What did he say? I'm sure it was something nasty.'

'Well.' I coughed, nervously. 'He said that you were different.'

She moved a little closer to me. 'In what way?'

'I don't know. Just different. He didn't go into detail. I don't think he really knew what he was talking about.'

'Well, I am different.' Marnie leaned forward and winked at me. 'Very different.'

She stood and picked up a writing pad from on top of the TV. 'Right, Dylan. Before we start, I have some questions for you. Are you okay to answer?'

I took a nervous sip of my lemonade and waited for the inevitable question that Valerie had warned me about. 'I'm okay,' I said.

'First. You're a glam-rock boy. What is your opinion of Garry Glitter?'

It wasn't the question I'd expected, but it was easy to answer. 'He's a gimmick. Glitter is not glam-rock.'

She smiled at me so generously. It was at that moment that I realised how beautiful Marnie Smith was, and that I was in love with her. 'That is such a great answer, Dylan. Next question. The Monkees? Good or bad?'

I'd watched the Monkees' TV show and enjoyed it, but didn't fancy them as musicians. 'They're okay, I suppose.'

She pointed the writing pad at me. 'Wrong answer, Dylan. Listen to this.' She put a forty-five single on the turntable, '(I'm Not Your) Steppin' Stone'. As the record played she danced around the room. I was spellbound.

When the song was over she came and stood on the couch and looked down at me. 'One day in the future,' she declared, 'the genius of the Monkees and their mastery of the three-minute pop song will be known to the music world.'

She sat down beside me. 'Final question, Dylan.' I waited. And waited. 'Are your parents psychic?' she asked.

'Pardon?'

'Your mum and dad, are they psychic?'

'No. My dad's a garbo, and Mum works behind the counter at the drycleaners.'

'Hmmm. I have been wondering about this. Your name is Dylan, and I just thought that when they named you maybe your parents were predicting the arrival of Bob Dylan at some time in the future.' She pressed her face to mine. The tip of my nose touched hers. 'Is that possible?'

I swallowed nervously. 'I don't think so.'

'Do you like Bob Dylan?' she asked.

'Not really. He's a little complicated for me.'

Marnie was so beautiful, and there was no doubt I'd fallen deeply in love for the first time in my life. But she was also crazy. The afternoon was not going to plan. Not my plan, or Valerie and Lisa's.

Marnie sensed my apprehension. She took me by the hand. 'I'm sorry for being silly, Dylan. I'm just nervous. Please come with me.'

We walked through the flat into her bedroom. The walls were decorated with music posters, mostly album covers. She pushed me gently onto the bed and curled up next to me. She put a hand against my ribbed jumper. 'I love this. It's beautiful.'

'Thank you.'

She twirled a lock of my hair between two fingers. 'It looks like a girl's top. With your hair so long, you look like a girl, a little.' Before I could protest she added, 'I like that, the way you look. I think you're beautiful. Wait.' She leaned across to her dresser and picked up a mascara stick. 'Open your eyes wide and do as I say.'

'Why?'

'Do you want a kiss, Dylan?'

'Yes. I want a kiss,' I said, impressed with my own boldness.

She applied mascara to my eyelashes and then coloured my cheeks with rouge. 'I like you this way,' she said. 'You can kiss me now.' I leaned forward, a little too eagerly.

She lifted a finger. 'Slow and soft, Dylan.'

We kissed, as light as a butterfly, I would later reflect about that moment.

'That was so nice,' she said. 'But we need something more.' She reached across to her dresser again.

'Lipstick?' I asked.

'Yes,' she said. 'The colour is *Son Amour*. It's French.'

'What does it mean?' I asked, as Marnie coloured my lips.

'His love. Her love. It can mean either. Both. That's why I like it.'

Marnie sat back and admired her work. 'Oh, you really are lovely.' She ran her hands through her hair and pushed it back. Marnie looked very different all of a sudden. 'We can kiss now,' she said. 'A real kiss.'

We kissed. Deeply. I concentrated on keeping my tongue firmly in my mouth.

When we finished, Marnie's lips were smeared with *Son Amour*. 'That was so nice,' she said. 'Did you like it, Dylan?' I was incapable of answering. 'Would you like to kiss again? For real? We can more than kiss, if you like. Would you like that?'

'Yes, please,' was all I could manage.

'Okay.' She kissed me lightly on both cheeks. 'But before we do, I have one final question. The *big* question. Are you ready?'

All I wanted to do was kiss Marnie again. And touch her. I had to give the correct answer.

'Dylan.' She brushed hair away from my face. 'Dylan,' she repeated. 'The Beatles or The Rolling Stones. *That* is the question.'

I took Marnie's hands in mine and hoped for the best. 'Bowie,' I said. 'David Bowie.'

THE BLOOD BANK: A LOVE STORY

THE CITY STREETS WERE DESERTED except for a few of the homeless, an empty tram gliding by like a ghost ship and a sole busker working in the mall, a tin at his feet. He wore a cowboy outfit and wailed a suitably sorrowful Hank Williams standard. I was on my way to visit the blood bank for the first time.

Earlier that morning the prime minister had announced that 'difficult times call for heroes, heroes in the spirit of the Anzacs'. Well, I'd never been a hero and no-one in my family had been to war, voluntarily or otherwise, so my chances of stepping up for the nation were slim. Although, providing half a litre of my blood to the Red Cross did offer such an opportunity, as *now* was the time to stand up and be counted, according to the organisation itself.

Walking further on I noticed a homeless man wearing an expensive-looking three-piece suit sitting outside a locked and bolted department store. He asked if I had any spare change and I dropped a $1 coin in a baseball cap sitting on the footpath.

'Do you have a cigarette to go with it by any chance?' he asked.

I'd quit smoking six months earlier. 'Sorry, I don't have any.'

'Would you like one, then?' He pulled two bent cigarettes and a box of matches out of his shirt pocket. For no logical reason, the opportunity for a few minutes of social interaction with a stranger was suddenly appealing, as was the thought of a cigarette. He introduced himself as Rex, lit both cigarettes and passed one to me. I hesitated before putting the cigarette in my mouth, not wanting to offend Rex's hospitality.

'That's a nice suit you're wearing, Rex,' I offered.

'Yeah. Some city accountant fleeing to the coast gave it to me.' He scratched his bare chest. 'I wouldn't mind a shirt to go with it.'

'And a tie?'

'Yeah. A nice silk tie with flowers on it.'

Rex had a sign resting in his lap, written on cardboard in marker pen. It told his brief story of woe.

Please Help – I need to get to Queensland – I have sick children waiting for me.

I opened my wallet and dropped a $5 note in Rex's cap. 'How many kids do you have, Rex?'

He took a thoughtful drag on his cigarette and contemplated the question. 'I don't have any kids, mate.'

'But your sign, it says that you have sick children in Queensland.'

He looked wide-eyed at the sign, as if noticing it for the first time. 'I've never set foot in Queensland. Been single all my life. Take a look at me. No woman would have me.'

I looked down at my $5 note, eager to retrieve it. 'But that sign – isn't this robbery? Deception?'

Rex threw his head back and laughed. 'Of course it's not. I'm doing good by the community with this story.'

I took a drag of my cigarette, in search of an explanation. 'How's that work?'

'Well, just now, you gave me a dollar. Then you saw my little sign and you dropped another five. Why'd you do that?'

'Because you're supposed to have sick kiddies and you want to get home to them. I felt sorry for you.'

'Right!' he said, clapping his hands together. 'And if I hadn't said a word just now, confessed to you, you'd have walked away feeling real good about yourself, giving money for a good cause, that sort of shit. And I'd have a fiver in my pocket towards a feed.' He winked at me. 'That's a win–win, son.'

'But none of it's true.'

'But it is. All of it except the bit about the sick kids. And that hardly matters if we're both happy.'

I scratched my head, trying to make sense of his remarks.

'Where you off to?' he asked.

'To the Red Cross, to give blood.'

'Oh, good lad. I offered to donate one time, I thought there might be money in it. Turns out they were only offering a cheese sandwich for a pint. Didn't seem like a fair trade at all. As it was they knocked me back anyway. I don't reckon my blood could save the life of a street rat. You look fit and healthy though. They'll fancy your blood, once they see you. The nurse will likely suck it straight out of your jugular with her fangs. That will be two good deeds in one day for you. You'll be beside yourself with joy tonight.'

The blood bank was on the first floor of a high-rise office building. In the foyer I was handed an iPad by a nurse and instructed to answer a series of questions – *Yes or No answers only.* The first questions related to my health, the illnesses and diseases I'd never experienced, followed by the exotic countries I'd never visited, the tattoos and piercings I'd never had and the cocktail of illicit drugs I managed to avoid throughout my life. The final questions referenced my sexual history, including information about sex with other men, anal sex and 'vigorous' sex with sex workers. I completed the form and scrolled through my responses. I'd answered 'No' forty-two times out of forty-two questions. Never before had the mundane nature of my life been so starkly revealed.

A nurse guided me to a cubicle where I was asked to verify my answers. By the time we reached question forty-two she looked at me with pity; even she was bored. 'Have you given blood before?' she asked.

'No. This will be my first time.'

'Then this might be exciting for you. I promise not to hurt.'

Five minutes later I was looking down at my bare arm. A needle inserted into a vein delivered blood through a clear tube into a plastic bag. The procedure was over in less than ten minutes.

The nurse bandaged my arm and led me to a recovery area where I was able to make myself a drink and have something to eat. There wasn't a cheese sandwich in sight. A woman, most likely a little younger than me, sat at a table drinking coffee and eating a muffin.

'There are no sausage rolls,' she said.

'Pardon?'

'The warmer on the shelf there, it's on the blink. There's no pies, pasties or sausage rolls today. If I'd known, I would have waited and come in when they'd fixed it.'

I made myself a cup of tea and sat at the next table. 'Is this your first time here?' I asked.

'God, no,' she said. 'I've been donating for years.' She pointed to a small badge on the lapel of her cardigan. 'This is a lifetime achievement badge. Ten years of service to the community. I wouldn't know the number of lives that I've personally saved.' She closed her eyes and appeared to be doing a mental calculation. 'It must be in the hundreds.'

She flicked her hair away from her face in a manner that, to my surprise, quickened my pulse.

'You're a real hero,' I said, without knowing why.

'Yes, I suppose I am.' She smiled. 'But I wouldn't be one to boast about it. We need to think of each other, work together as a community and be considerate of others at this terrible time. Compassion. It's all we have.'

I was desperate to continue the conversation but didn't know what to say.

'How are the muffins?' I asked.

She looked at hers with disdain. 'Stale.'

We sat quietly gazing up at a television screen on the wall and watched the news on the pandemic. A woman had been caught stealing roast chickens from a food bank set aside for the needy. She was being escorted into a police station. She covered her face with a jacket, hiding from an angry crowd hurling abuse.

'Should cut her hands off,' my blood bank companion offered.

'I beg your pardon?'

She took a decent gouge out of her stale muffin. 'Stealing at a time like this. I'd cut both her hands off and give her life in prison.'

'Really?'

'No, not really.' She laughed. 'Just one hand would do.' She stood up. 'Have you finished your tea?'

I stared into the bottom of my empty cup. 'Yes.'

She again flicked her hair from her face. 'Maybe we could head out together? Go for a stroll? See where a walk takes us?'

I thought back to my forty-two negative responses on the questionnaire. I'd answered 'no' enough times for one day. 'Sure,' I said, throwing caution to the wind.

She took me by the hand.

'What about distancing?' I asked.

'Don't worry yourself. We can get inventive with that.'

THE DEATH OF MICHAEL McGUIRE

M OST EVERYONE ON THE STREET knew it would happen, and soon. Mick Mac, he knew only too well, as did his wife and children. Nobody was told directly. That's not the way of the world around here. But we knew. Even the young ones picked up on the signs. The street was quiet and waiting. A man could smell it. The pillow talk went up a volume also. Husbands and wives whispering in the dark, the women controlling the show in the bed, naturally. It got me every time, as my wife of twenty years, Cate, was a world champion of the mattress.

Although she was the boss of the show upstairs, she took the conversation too far at the tea table one night. I understood why, but it didn't make it right. She was best friends with Mick Mac's wife, Louise, and had been for most of her life. They'd been at the convent school together and started work on the same day, house-maiding in a city hotel. They'd also lived on the same street – this street – since they were kids. Maybe Mick Mac put Louise up to it, asking Cate to make enquiries through me. I can't be certain about that. Either way, Cate should have known better. Downstairs was not the place for such talk.

'Is there a way out for him?' she asked me, pouring my cup of tea at the table after we'd eaten.

I tensed and shovelled two spoons of sugar into my cup. 'What are you talking about? A way out of what?'

She looked across at our fifteen-year-old, Margie. 'Go to your room, please, love. I need to speak with your father. This is something private, between us.'

Margie picked up her cup and looked briefly at me. Even she, a girl still in school, knew what this so-called private business was about.

'You know what I'm asking about, Frank. Don't play your games with me,' Cate said.

'I do know. But why would you be asking?' I said. 'This is not our business, never has been, and you know so.'

'I know, I know. But I'm thinking about Louise and the three kids. They won't be able to pay the rent and have no place to go.'

I drank from my sweetened cup of tea. 'They'll be taken care of. That's been the way, always. A Sunday barrel will be put on. There'll be a collection as well. They won't be left behind.'

Cate let out her ponytail and shook her mane of hair. It settled on her shoulders. She was such a good-looking woman. 'He's a husband and a father, Frank. Can't something be done?'

I glared at her. She knew there was nothing that could be done, and she knew better than me that interference, even a plea for mercy, might be met with broken bones.

'You'd put us in danger, woman? Me, you and our daughter?

I can't do anything for Mick Mac. Or his wife and family. He should have thought about his own people before he put his hand in the till. It was thousands that he took. Thousands, Cate. From under their nose, the same people who bring money into these streets.'

Cate stood up, untied her apron and threw it on the table. 'It's dishonest money. It's always been dishonest. Gambling, grog and women. It's not the sort of money we need. It causes more misery than good.'

'I don't care. That's not at stake here. The money, good or bad, has kept Mick Mac's family well fed and cared for. He's enjoyed the earn. Too much as it turns out. And he went and fucked it up.'

'When?' she asked.

'What do you mean, when?'

'When will it happen?'

I slammed a hand on the table in frustration. 'I don't know. Please, Cate, don't you ask me again. We're not to talk about this.'

The truth was the street had little idea of when Mick Mac would be killed and how. But the matter wouldn't linger, that was certain. Tardiness was a bad look for the men who Mick Mac had wronged. If the matter dragged on, it could send a message that the big boys were getting soft in their old age. How and where it would be done was uncertain, although there were standard rules that applied. A man shot opening his own front door to a death knock was common, but in Mick Mac's case, with three kiddies in the house, such a situation would be avoided. Shooting a man in front of his own family was frowned on, unless he'd dogged to the police, of course. In such circumstances the entire family might be blown up. Or the same fella could be dragged from the home and shot in the street. Put on a bit of a show for the neighbours. That wouldn't be Mick Mac's fate. He was a robber, but never a lagger.

Word had got around that one of the bookies up on the hill was running a line of bets on the timing of Mick Mac's exit. As distasteful as it appeared, the story was likely true. With money to be made on the street, sentiment couldn't stand in the way.

Personally, I'd always got on well with Mick. We'd even done a little side business together one time. He was friendly enough and harmless, until he fell into gambling himself. Cards. He was on a good wage, running the pick-up for the SP syndicate. The word was that he lined his pockets of a Saturday afternoon and lost the lot the same night at a baccarat club across the other side of the city. There was talk of women too, which came as no surprise. If there was one habit I couldn't abide in Mick Mac, it was that his eyes lingered far too long on Cate whenever she stopped to talk with Louise on the street. He'd also been seen sitting in cafes here and there, with different barmaids from a few pubs around the traps. My own dad, who'd never exactly been father of the year, gave me little advice in life except, *Keep your head down* and *Women and the punt, both can end you.*

Up in our bedroom that night, Cate glared at me when I walked into the room. She was seated in front of the dresser brushing her hair. I said nothing, got into bed and rifled through a stack of comic Westerns, settling on a title suitable for the occasion:

The Gun and the Knife. I sat up in bed reading and smoking. Cate got in beside me, turned her back and slammed her head theatrically into the pillow. The matter was not over for her.

I butted my cigarette in the ashtray and lay down. I could hear a tram rattling past, two streets away.

'Frank,' she whispered.

'What is it now?'

'I know there's nothing that can be done.'

'Good,' I said.

'But …'

'But, what?'

She turned around to face me and began unbuttoning her nightie. 'When it's over and done, you be the one to run the barrel for him. We can do it here in the yard. And you get a good singer in. There'll be more money in the hat for the kids that way. And be sure the butcher supplies the best cuts of meat.'

'Jesus, Cate. Is that all? You want me to fucking tap-dance for him?'

'No, that's not all.'

As the bedroom was Cate's domain, I bit my tongue. 'What else do you want from me?'

'I want you to stand up and speak good of him at the funeral. I want his three children to hear that their father was a good man.'

'Come on, Cate,' I whispered. 'He's not all good. Mick Mac is a thief. And from the wrong people.'

'Don't be silly, Frank. That's only bad judgement around here, not a sign of poor character. Will you do that for Louise and the kids?'

'I don't know that I can do all of it.'

Cate slipped a warm hand between my legs. 'But you can, Frank. I believe in you.'

The tension went up a few notches, and the street was about to crack open. Walking the footpath itself became an exercise in caution. Some wore slippers to protect their footsteps from being heard. Ted Hawkins's vicious dog, Saint, wouldn't even raise a yelp from the bottle yard lest he be shot for disturbing the peace. Avoidance included a restriction on conversation. All of a sudden, each one of us, men and women, old and young, became fascinated by the peculiarities of the weather.

'It's a nice enough morning,' I said to Jim Hart, passing him on the corner outside the bank.

'Yes,' he said, 'although it might come down later in the day.'

I looked up at the clear blue sky. 'Oh, you think so, Jimmy? Well, you may be right. I'll get back to you.' I smiled.

Talk was had about politics, sick kiddies, the slim chance of the outsider in the last race of the day getting up, even chat about the best time to put tomato seedlings in the ground. What none of us spoke about was Mick Mac's predicament.

That was until I saw Louise up the street, walking home from the grocer, carrying a parcel under one arm and chewing on the fingernails of her other hand. She stopped on the footpath, blocking my way. The poor woman had dark rings under her eyes. If she'd slept over the last week it couldn't have been for long.

'Louise,' I said, feeling flush in the cheeks.

She grabbed hold of me. The woman couldn't have looked more desperate. 'Frank. He has only one chance – you. You have to speak up for him. People respect you around here. You can put in a word for him, let *them* know he's sorry and that he'll pay them back. Mick's a good worker. He'll get a job, on shift, and pay them back with extras. You have to tell them that. Please, Frank. We can't lose him.' Louise was about to break down. She gripped me by the arm with both hands. Being seen on the street with her, comforting her, would be a strike against me.

'I can't do that, Louise. I've got no sway with them. As it is, they already know they can get the money back. Work your Mick into his grave. It would be the easy way out. It's not money. This is about order and respect.' I pushed her away, with just enough force. 'I told Cate to let you know that I'll be sure you're taken care of and that I'll speak on his behalf. But not now. Afterwards.'

She turned wild on me, which I wouldn't hold against her under the circumstances. 'You're a coward, Frank. Nothing but a coward. All you fellas standing by to see another man, one of your own, shot dead in the street.' She spat on the ground at my feet. 'I hate the lot of you.'

I raised my hands in surrender. Yes, I was a coward. There was no doubt about that. But a live one.

That night, after tea, Cate was in the yard with the washing. She heard someone bang on the back gate. Such a knock was never welcome and signalled the arrival of illegal activity, an unwelcome visitor, or both. She came into the kitchen, nervously patting both hands to her cheeks. 'There's someone to see you.'

'Who is it?'

'Michael McGuire.'

Mick Mac was pacing the yard, between the toilet and our dogless kennel. He looked unwell and all weedy.

I tried keeping the conversation jovial, which may not have suited the walking dead. 'How are you doing, Mick? You've faded away to a shadow. You'll be fighting flyweight at Festival Hall the way you're heading.'

Mick Mac continued pacing like he hadn't heard a word I'd said. 'What are you after, Mick?' I asked. 'It's near bedtime for me.'

'You need to do something for me, Frank.'

I thought *fuck*, now the corpse himself is going to plead. 'I'm sorry, Mick. I told your missus, there's nothing I can do for you. I'm not even a soldier. They won't listen to me. Worse still, I could come out with injuries. Permanently damaged. I'm a labourer, all my life, Mick. If I'm not fit for the job, I'm fucked. Me and the family.'

'It's not that, Frank. I know that. It's too late for me. Your Cate spoke to Louise about what will happen afterwards. Your offer. I'm grateful for that. Truly, Frank.' He handed me a crumpled sheet of paper. 'This is what I want.'

I opened the sheet. A list, scrawled in ink. 'What's this?'

'What I want done and said at my funeral.'

Mick Mac's funeral list was a mix of popular songs, prayers, eulogies and toasts to a dead man's body.

'There's a lot here, Mick,' I said. 'This will take some time. It could create restlessness with the crowd.'

'No, no,' Mick said. 'This includes the wake. Not only the church. You save the speeches for the wake.'

'Oh, I see. *Danny Boy.* Who do you want for that?'

'Oh, Rory at The Brickmakers pub. He has the loveliest voice. Do you think we can get him?'

I wasn't sure that we could. Rory Cleary was constantly in demand as a singer for weddings, funerals and the occasional christening. 'I'm sure we can get Rory for you,' I lied. 'He's a good man. He'll do this. No doubt.'

Mick continued to shuffle about nervously. 'Is there something more I can ask of you, Frank?'

I'd had enough. 'No more, please, Mick. You'll have a great send-off and I can promise you the pot will be full for Louise and the children. That's the best I can do. But not more. Except the singer, of course.'

'It's not that, Frank. Not that at all.'

'What then?'

'Are you still holding that handgun? The pistol.'

I thought Mick might have forgotten about the gun. I certainly had. Three years had gone by since I came by the weapon. The last time someone had knocked at the back gate it was one of the Baxter brothers, Ron, who'd been renting two doors along from us as a front for fencing stolen goods. Ron was a menace and very unpopular. That night, he handed me a pillowcase and said, 'Hold on to this for me. I'll be back for it.' As soon as he left, I looked in the pillowcase. It contained a pistol and a handful of bullets. Ron never returned for the gun. He was on the run for armed robbery when he was shot dead by the dogs.

Handguns were hard to come by and were traded for good money, so a week after Ron's death I walked the pillowcase up the laneway behind our row of terraces and showed the contents to Mick, who could move most anything at a price. He quickly found a buyer with a decent offer. But when it came time to part with the gun, I changed my mind.

'I think I'll hang on to it,' I told him.

Mick was bemused. 'Why, Frank? You're no crook.'

I wasn't sure why I no longer wanted to part company with the gun. 'Who knows, Mick. Maybe it will come in handy one day. I'll keep it for insurance.'

'Are you still holding the handgun?' Mick repeated. 'I need it.'

'No, you don't. You can't fight the big boys off with a handgun, Mick,' I said.

'It's not for them. It's for me.'

Once his words had set in, I sighed. 'Come on, Mick, you don't want to do that to yourself. Jesus.'

'Fuck off, Frank. You and the rest of them, you can fuck off. You're all waiting for me to be shot. But me, I have no say in the matter, when or where. Fuck that. Give me the gun. Please. I don't want to be sitting in the dark in the front room any longer, waiting for this to happen. Louise is a wreck. If this isn't over soon she'll be in no state to care for the kids. Please, Frank. It's not a lot to ask. I know I fucked up and now I want to walk my own way out.'

I opened the rusting door on the old wood stove in the corner of the shed, reached in and brought out the pillowcase. It was pitted with small holes where the rats had been at it. I pushed the pillowcase to Mick Mac's chest. 'You best go,' I said, too weak to look him in the eye. I felt angry, not at Mick, but myself. I was an arsehole. We'd all behaved like arseholes.

Later, I lay in bed in the dark, Cate resting her head on my chest. 'What did he want out there?'

'Mick Mac?'

'Who else,' she said. 'Yeah, Mick Mac.'

'Nothing you need to be worrying over. He just wanted a chat.'

'His life is in danger, and he takes the risk of leaving the house for a chat with you? I'm not silly, Frank.'

'I never said you were, Cate. But you are a nosy woman at times.'

She ran a hand down the side of my body. 'What might it take for a confession from you?'

The sound of a single gunshot woke me in the dead of night. I sat up in bed, unsure of what I'd heard, or if I'd really heard anything at all. Perhaps it was a nightmare I'd woken from? Cate stirred, turned over and fell back to sleep.

It was Louise McGuire's scream, heard along the street, that announced Mick Mac had been shot by his own hand. If the big boys had done it, Louise would have wailed quietly, with sadness and even some relief. Her chilling scream was an expression of shock.

The bullet entered Mick Mac's body under his jaw. It exited through his left eye. How the bullet never killed him became folklore along the street. A miracle, literally, according to Louise, who later told Cate that she'd knelt by her bed morning and night and prayed for the life of her wayward husband. 'I prayed until my knees were fucking crippled. And thank Christ the Lord, He finally heard me.'

Mick Mac was in the hospital for more than a month, two weeks in a coma. When he returned to the street, he carried a limp courtesy of a bullet fragment permanently lodged in his brain and wore a glass eye, a slightly lighter brown than his good eye. He looked a sorry sight, and not a soul on the street knew what would happen next. We were in uncharted waters, a marked man coming back from the dead. Mick Mac himself didn't seem too concerned. He walked the streets with a sense of abandon. The man actually whistled, as if he'd been given a second life, which he had, at least temporarily.

Again, we waited. To the surprise of all, a month later the man was back at his old job, running the SP book, ensuring that everyone who needed to weigh in with the correct cash at the end of the day did so. Cate told me that Louise told her that Mick Mac went to Confession, washed his sins from his grubby soul, and swore off other women and the cards for life. By putting a gun to his own head, Mick Mac had remarkably pulled off a win-win. He was alive and gainfully employed, and those who ran the street, rather than come out of the affair looking soft, were seen to have acted with benevolence in allowing Mick Mac to carry on. Several times, Cate had badgered me at the tea table about my backyard conversation with him on the night that he shot himself. I refused to give her a word. Until she took the conversation upstairs.

THE MANGER

The first Sunday in December was marked in red pen on a calendar hanging on the back of the kitchen door. Kathy wasn't tall enough to reach the calendar so she'd dragged a chair across the floor, climbed on it and circled the number five. She then stood in the centre of the room studying the number, transfixed, willing the date to rush towards her.

In the following weeks, as the date approached, she sat at the table drawing her own version of the nativity scene: the Virgin Mary, Joseph, the Three Wise Men, farm animals and, of course, the Baby Jesus, dressed in a jumpsuit and bib.

Raeleen, Kathy's older sister, teased her about the drawing. 'You know, he wouldn't be wearing all that stuff, the baby, not back then, in the olden days. A jumpsuit?'

'I don't care,' Kathy said. 'We're not in the olden days, Rae. Look at the date.'

Raeleen pointed to a drawing of an indistinguishable animal. 'What's that animal there, by Joseph's feet?'

'It's a rabbit.'

'You can't have a rabbit in the nativity. They never had rabbits over there when Jesus was a baby. It would be too hot for a rabbit.'

'They did have rabbits,' Kathy replied. 'Uncle Cal says that rabbits are like God, they're everywhere.'

'Not in the Bible, they're not.'

'How would you know?'

'Because I got a hundred out of a hundred for Catechism. Three years in a row. I've never had a question about a rabbit and I've never seen one in the Bible. That's how I know.' Raeleen leaned forward and whispered in her younger sister's ear. 'And if you want my opinion, there wasn't any Virgin Mary either.'

'No Virgin Mary! Don't you say that!'

Raeleen wasn't finished with teasing her sister. 'Well, maybe there was a Mary. But a virgin?'

Their mother walked into the kitchen, wrapped in a chenille dressing-gown, hair in rollers and fluffy pink slippers. She could have been walking onto the set of a suburban soap opera. She noticed the look of shock and flushed cheeks on her youngest daughter's face.

'Don't you be whispering lies into that girl's ear, Raeleen Maree. What did your sister say to you, Kathy?'

'That there are no rabbits in the Bible.' Kathy snivelled. 'Is that true?'

'That can't be all your sister said in order to turn your cheeks to beetroot. What else did she say?'

Kathy didn't want to contemplate the consequences of what Raeleen had said, let alone repeat the words to her mother.

The thought alone, that Jesus' own mother, Mary, wasn't a virgin, was a sin of itself.

'What did she say?' their mother insisted.

'I said to her,' Raeleen answered, 'that, if she's lucky, Father Keegan will pick her out to help with the nativity scene.'

'And that's all you said? By the look on her face, I would think your sister has been shocked by the devil.'

'There was no devil.' Raeleen nudged her sister. 'You're just excited, aren't you, Kathy?'

'Yes,' Kathy replied. 'That's all she said, Mum.'

Whenever Kathy wanted to ask her older sister a serious question, she waited until they were in bed at night, after the light had been turned out. Kathy slept in the bottom bunk, Raeleen on the top. Kathy drew the bedspread and blankets away from her body, lifted a leg and rattled on the wooden slats of the mattress above her head.

'Are you asleep, Raeleen?'

'Yep, and I'm having a beautiful dream, so please don't interrupt me.'

'Can I ask you a question?'

'Let me ask you one. Could I stop you asking a question if I really wanted to?'

Kathy sat up in bed. 'Tomorrow, Father Keegan is going to choose the students to help with the nativity.'

'That's not a question, Kath. We call that a fact,' Raeleen said. 'He's been doing that since the days of the Ark.'

'Who do you think he'll pick?'

117

'I don't have a clue and I don't care. All I know is that it will be one of the goody-goodies. That's what Father Keegan does. He goes for the quiet ones. And the best behaved.'

'Why didn't the Father pick you in your year?'

'Like I just said, he picked the best behaved, and the smartest. He was never going to pick me. That was the year I smashed the tuckshop window with the netball and got caught sneaking out of the Confession line. I'm glad that I was never picked.'

'Why? All the girls I know want to be chosen for the nativity. They'll get to sit in the front row at Mass next Sunday and stand up in front of the whole church. You didn't want that?'

Raeleen laughed out loud. 'Being forced to go to Mass each Sunday is bad enough without being paraded around by the Father. You want it, don't you, to be picked?'

Being chosen for the nativity scene was all Kathy had wanted since starting school, but not because she wanted the attention of the Sunday congregation. She'd fallen in love with the Baby Jesus, the moment she first saw him lying in the wooden crib on a bed of straw, looking up at his mother, Mary.

'I don't really care if the Father picks me or not,' she said.

'That's such a lie, Kathy. You should be sent to Confession for what you've just said. Father Keegan will give you three Hail Marys for that one sin alone.'

'Hey, Rae?'

'Hey, what?'

'Do you really believe that Mother Mary isn't a virgin?'

'Why don't you ask Father Keegan while you're at Confession. He'll send you off with a full rosary and a visit to the stations of the cross.'

The following morning students assembled in the narrow hall next to the bluestone church. Each child sat quietly, girls on one side of the hall, boys on the other. The nuns sat together on the platform at the front of the hall, silent statues dressed in the white habits and gowns of summer. Father Keegan, tall and broad-shouldered, a mass of silver hair reaching for the ceiling, waited until the room quietened and fell silent.

As he spoke he tapped the back of one hand with the fingers of the other. 'Today is a special day on the yearly calendar for both the school and church,' he began, the same words he used each year. 'Today we choose the six students who have shown, both in the classroom and in their own hearts, a profound love of God.'

'Amen,' the hall thundered.

Kathy watched the Father as he paced the platform, nervously pulling on one of her plaits.

'Today I choose the students who will assist me in arranging our annual nativity scene in the church garden for the Christmas season. But firstly …' The Father paused and inspected the students' eager faces. 'Firstly,' he repeated, 'we remember today that the nativity scene represents the most significant day on the Catholic calendar, the birth of Jesus Christ.'

'Amen.'

The Father stepped down from the platform and stood on the girls' side of the hall. Kathy, seated in the second row, followed his movements closely.

'Through the nativity scene,' he said, 'we celebrate the life of the Immaculate Virgin Mary.' He appeared to look directly at Kathy.

She was reminded of Raeleen's comment the night before, and her own questioning of Mary's purity. She dropped her head, terrified that he could read her mind.

The Father raised both arms above his head. 'We celebrate the Immaculate Conception. And we celebrate the birth of the Virgin's son.' He walked along the centre aisle separating the girls from the boys. 'Is there anything in our lives more sacred than the Baby Jesus?' he asked.

'No!' came the refrain.

'Do we worship the Baby Jesus?'

'Yes!'

'Do we worship all babies?'

'Yes!'

He marched back to the front of the room, turned and raised his arms again. 'Are not all newborn our sacred gift?'

'Yes, Father!'

He stepped back onto the platform. Sister Josephine, the head nun from the school, stood and handed the Father a sheet of paper. He held it in the air.

'The six children on this list will come to the sacristy after the school bell.'

The first name read out was Margaret Hunter. Kathy was not surprised. Margaret was the top student in her year, her mother volunteered at the church cleaning the altar, and Margaret was already a favourite of the Father's. On Ash Wednesday, earlier in the year, she'd been chosen to veil the statues in the church with the purple cloth that hid the faces of saints from view until being released on Easter Sunday. The following morning at school she'd lifted her golden fringe and displayed the ash cross that Father Keegan had marked her forehead with.

'It will never leave me,' she solemnly announced.

'Only if you never wash your face,' Raeleen had said. 'And then you'll stink.'

Margaret Hunter left her chair in the front row, walked up onto the platform and stood behind the Father. As each child's name was called Kathy prayed that her own name would be next. But she wasn't called. After the name of the sixth student was read out, all students stood and applauded. Kathy looked into the eyes of each of the chosen students and thought again about the Baby Jesus. She was convinced that none of the girls and boys standing on the platform could love and care for Jesus as much as she did.

That night at home she refused to eat her tea. Her grandmother, who visited the house once a week, sat across from Kathy at the table. Her usual habit was to speak about her granddaughters to their mother, without uttering a word directly to the girls themselves.

'What's wrong with Kathy?' she asked her daughter.

'There's nothing wrong with her, Mum.'

'There is something wrong with her,' Raeleen piped up.

'And what would that be?' her grandmother asked.

'This morning at assembly, Father Keegan read out the names of those to help with the nativity scene. She wanted to be on the list, but her name wasn't called. She loves the Baby Jesus. She thinks he's her own baby, don't you, Kathy?'

Kathy lashed out and kicked Raeleen under the table on the shin.

'Hey, watch it!' Raeleen screamed.

'Stop it!' their mother demanded. 'There's over three hundred children in that school. They can't pick you all,' she explained to Kathy. 'Perhaps you'll be chosen next year?'

'Don't let her worry about this year or the next,' her grandmother said. 'She is fortunate for not being picked.'

'Why is that?' Raeleen asked, genuinely curious.

'Don't be asking such a question,' her mother interrupted. 'Your grandmother is being mischievous, as usual.'

Raeleen insisted on asking the question again. 'Why is she lucky, Nanna?'

Kathy jumped up from her chair and ran out of the room.

'You're not staying for dessert?' Raeleen called after her sister. 'Can I have your slice of pie?' She then asked the question a third time.

'You'll need to ask your mother,' her grandmother responded. 'And I need to mind my tongue,' she added, not that she meant a word of it.

The following Sunday a crowd gathered around the nativity scene before eleven o'clock Mass. The life-sized statues of the Three Wise Men stood to one side, under a peppercorn tree, with their offerings. Kathy thought they looked tired. The statue of the donkey, which Raeleen believed wore the saddest face she'd ever seen on an animal, stared blankly at the gathered crowd. The Virgin Mary and Joseph stood either side of the crib. The Virgin, dressed resplendently in a powder-blue veil and gown, clasped her hands together in prayer. Joseph wore a fawn tunic and held a hammer in one hand. Between them, resting in the bed of straw, lay the Baby Jesus. He was made of solid plaster and tipped the scales at a world-record weight for a newborn. Jesus wore a white crocheted gown, designed and knitted by one of the nuns many years earlier. A wooden collection box sat on a tree stump next to the crib. The parent of any child who wanted to have their photograph taken with Jesus was expected to offer a donation.

Kathy stood behind Raeleen, watching as children came forward, one by one, and sat in the bed of straw next to Baby Jesus. Although the Father had ordered that no child was permitted to touch the Baby, some children could not help but caress Jesus, and even plant a kiss on his lips.

'Can't see any rabbits,' Raeleen quipped to her sister. 'Do you want to have your picture taken?'

'We don't have a camera,' Kathy said.

'It doesn't matter. I can get someone else to take it for you. I can see Mrs Mead from the tuckshop holding a camera. We can ask her.'

'I don't want my picture taken. Leave me alone.'

Kathy had waited so long to be chosen to help with the nativity scene. She felt cheated. She observed Margaret Hunter, expecting to see a self-satisfied smile on her face. But Margaret didn't seem happy at all. In fact, she looked miserable. Raeleen also noticed her sombre face.

During the Mass, Father Keegan spoke again about the purity of the birth of Jesus and the need for His followers to protect the newborn *with every drop of Catholic blood*.

'What's he talking about?' Kathy asked her mother. 'Is there going to be a war or something?'

'Be quiet,' her mother ordered, as the Father added, as if on cue, 'We are at war on this matter of the sanctity of life and we cannot fail.'

When the six chosen students were introduced to the parishioners at the conclusion of Mass, each of them smiled, except for Margaret Hunter. She looked quite ill.

Raeleen cupped a hand over Kathy's ear and whispered, 'What's wrong with her. I think she's in some sort of shock.'

'I don't know,' Kathy whispered back. 'All I know is that she's being ungrateful.'

After Mass, the crowd around the nativity scene grew. More children waiting to have their photograph taken with the Baby Jesus, pushing and shoving each other. One of the Rizzo twins tried bunking his brother onto the back of the donkey. He tumbled over the other side, taking the animal with him. The sad-faced donkey fell on top of the boy, who began to cry. Seeing what his sons had done, their father slapped one twin across the back of the head, then dragged the other boy from under the donkey and gave him a whack also.

Kathy watched the chaos in horror, worried that Baby Jesus could be crushed in a stampede. 'This is awful.'

'Sure is,' Raeleen said. 'The donkey's tail has broken off. Father Keegan won't be happy about this.'

Kathy looked through the legs of the rowdy children to where Baby Jesus lay. She was sure she could see fear on his face and became distressed herself.

'Can we go home, Rae? I don't like being here.'

Raeleen noticed their mother talking to May Brown, an old friend of hers from the shirt factory they'd worked in when they were both newlyweds. 'Okay. Let's go. Mum will be here all day, talking.'

Kathy took a final look at the Baby Jesus and made the sign of the cross, praying for his safety.

'Did you see the look on Margaret Hunter's face, standing up there in front of the whole church,' Raeleen asked, as the pair walked home. 'She had a face like a smacked arse.'

'Don't swear like that.'

'Arse? It's hardly swearing. I can say worse than that.'

'Well, don't. I don't want to hear it.'

'Arse! Arse! Arse!' Raeleen screamed at the top of her voice.

That night Kathy again refused to eat, annoying her mother and providing Raeleen with yet another excuse to tease her sister about the Baby Jesus.

'She's jealous that some other girl is taking care of her baby.'

'I don't have a baby,' Kathy screamed. 'I'm only ten years old. I can't have a baby.'

Their mother put a stop to the argument and ordered Kathy to the corner shop. 'I need you to pick up a bag of coke for the boiler. Or we'll have no hot water for a bath in the morning.'

'But I can't carry those heavy bags. Send her,' she said, poking her tongue out at her older sister.

'I'm not sending Raeleen. I'm sending you. You look all wound up. The brisk air will settle you. Take the old baby carriage from the sideway. Barty Collins will lift the bag of coke into the carriage for you at the shop and I'll lift it out at this end.' She opened her purse and handed the money for the bag of fuel to Kathy, who went off to the shop.

Raeleen helped her mother tidy the kitchen and do the dishes.

'I want you to stop teasing your sister,' her mother said, handing her daughter a plate to dry.

'Do I really have to?' Raeleen said.

'Yes, you have to. She really wanted this, the nativity business, and I don't want her upsetting herself anymore. If she doesn't eat soon, she'll fade away to a shadow.'

'Did you see Margaret Hunter in church today?' Raeleen asked.

'Of course, I did. The Father called her name and she stood up there with the rest.'

'Did you see the look on her face then? It was like she was going to die.'

'Don't you be silly, Raeleen. The girl was being shy was all.'

'It was more than that,' Raeleen insisted. 'I bet you saw her, Mum?'

The next morning a crowd of children gathered in front of the nativity scene at the church garden. Some stood in stunned silence. Others, the younger kids, were crying.

'Something's going on,' Raeleen said to Kathy, crossing the street together. 'Let's go take a look.'

'Not me,' Kathy said.

The sisters parted. In the schoolyard Kathy saw Theresa Dove, a girl who sat next to her in class. Theresa's eyes were red raw.

'What's wrong?' Kathy asked.

'It's the Baby Jesus,' Theresa bawled.

'The Baby Jesus? What about him?'

'He's gone.'

'Gone? He can't be gone.'

'The Baby Jesus has been taken. Someone has kidnapped him.'

Kathy turned and looked towards the church where she could see Raeleen had pushed her way to the front of the crowd. Raeleen turned, saw her sister, left the crowd and joined Kathy in the yard. 'The Baby Jesus, he's gone,' she said. 'He's been stolen.'

'I know,' Kathy said.

'You know?' Raeleen remembered back to the previous night, when her sister had taken such a long time to return from the shop with the *baby carriage*. She grabbed her sister by the arm and guided her to a far corner of the schoolyard where no-one could hear them.

'Of course you know. You took him.' Raeleen was pleased. 'Yes! You stole the Baby Jesus.' She held Kathy and kissed her madly on both cheeks. 'I love you, little sister. You should see the expression on the Father's face. He looks like he's going to pass out.'

Kathy wrestled herself free. 'I didn't steal him. Are you crazy, Rae? Why would I steal the Baby Jesus?'

'Why? Because all you've ever wished for in life is the Baby Jesus. You wanted him all to yourself.'

The accusation shocked Kathy. 'I might have wanted the Baby, but not like that. No-one wants a baby *that* much.'

'Really?' Raeleen said. 'Really?'

'Yes. Really. You're crazy.'

Raeleen realised her sister was telling the truth. 'I thought you wanted the Baby Jesus more than anything in the world?'

'Not more than anything,' Kathy said, feeling suddenly wiser than her older sister. 'I might love the Baby Jesus, but I wouldn't steal him. That would be a sin.'

Theresa Dove ran across the yard towards the sisters. She was shouting hysterically, 'They found him, the Baby Jesus. They found him.'

'Where?' Raeleen asked.

'Buried,' Theresa said.

'Buried!' Raeleen and Kathy screamed in unison. 'Where?'

'He was buried in Margaret Hunter's back garden. Her mother was out this morning watering the rose garden and noticed the side of the Baby Jesus' face poking out of the soil.'

'My arse,' Raeleen said. 'You're making this up.'

'No, I'm not,' Theresa insisted. 'Nola Tracy, who lives next door to Margaret, was in her yard feeding her dog when she heard Mrs Hunter scream out. When she saw the face of Jesus, she thought it was a real baby. You know, like those ones they find sometimes?'

Every child in the school had heard the stories of abandoned babies, and spoke of them only in whispers.

'Where is Baby Jesus now?' Kathy asked.

'Well …' Theresa hesitated. 'They say that parts of him are missing, because Margaret smashed him into pieces with a hammer. Joseph's hammer. It was stolen too.'

'A hammer?' Kathy said, shaking her head. 'Why would she do that?'

'Baby Jesus is lucky she didn't flush him down the toilet,' Raeleen said. 'That's what they do when they don't want the abandoned babies. Put them in the toilet and flush the water.'

'What are you talking about now?' Kathy asked, horrified at the thought of a baby being flushed through water pipes.

'Anyway, he's not down the toilet,' Theresa said. 'The Father sent some boys from the top year to the Hunters' garden. They had shovels and rakes. They'll have to find the bits and pieces of the Baby Jesus and put him back together.'

'Just like Humpty Dumpty.' Raeleen laughed.

'That's not funny,' Theresa said.

'I know,' Raeleen replied, and laughed even louder. She couldn't stop.

'Your sister is mental,' Theresa said to Kathy. 'She's going to hell,' she added, before running back across the yard.

'Why would she do that?' Kathy asked her sister. 'Smash the Baby Jesus with a hammer and bury him in the garden?'

Raeleen thought about the look she'd seen on Margaret Hunter's face at Sunday Mass. She also remembered the words of her grandmother, that Kathy had been *lucky* that she wasn't chosen to help Father Keegan with the nativity scene. She stopped in the middle of the schoolyard, and was momentarily consumed by a thought so dark she wondered if it would be a sin to even think about it.

TOGETHER

M Y MOTHER CARED FOR MY grandmother, Elsie, every
day for the last ten years of her long life – feeding her,
washing her, listening to her petty complaints about the poor
quality of the television reception, and answering the same
question over and over with a degree of patience that wore
other family members down. She wouldn't hear of having Elsie
put into a nursing home, even after my grandmother wandered
out of her government flat one Christmas Day. Elsie wasn't
found until hours later, barefoot, wearing a thin cotton nightie
and wandering the streets of our old neighbourhood in the
darkness and unseasonal rain. The young couple who found
her told the police that Elsie had been crying out for her own
mother, a woman she'd never known.

At birth, Elsie had been taken from her mother and placed
in an orphanage, where she was given a new name but no
adoptive family to go with it. Elsie spent her early years
learning to *scrub floors until they shined*, she would tell me,

sitting at her table and enjoying the city's best roast dinner.

It was only when Nan became terminally ill that my mother gave up her struggle and allowed Elsie to be put in hospital. But she was adamant that a woman who'd provided a good life for others would not die alone. A family meeting was held and it was agreed – between a daughter, two sons, several cousins, grandchildren and a few close friends – that in the final weeks of Elsie's life at least one family member would be with her at all times. If she'd had her way, my mother would have sat at Elsie's bedside twenty-four hours a day, every day.

Fortunately, my older sister, Jennifer, persuaded her that we'd need to share the load, and drew up a roster. Jennifer had been creating lists and organising the people around her since she was a kid. It wasn't so much an older-sister thing – or at least not just that. Our mother was on her own for most of our childhood. My father went off to work one day and never came back. Mum's explanation to us was that he'd swapped her for *a newer model*, which made no sense to me at the time. It did mean that Jennifer took on a lot of responsibility from a young age. She never complained. I think she actually enjoyed it.

Elsie was admitted to a new wing of the same hospital where I'd been stitched back together and had bones mended many times as a child. I was a wild kid with an ability for finding innovative ways to test the limits of my body. As a consequence, I carried many war wounds – scars, old fractures and emotional damage. One scar, on my lower right leg, was the result of climbing onto my grandmother's roof when I was six and falling through the skylight above her bathroom. It was school holidays and my mother was working twelve-hour shifts at a shoe factory in Collingwood, so Elsie was taking care of me at the time. Nan was at the kitchen stove, making soup, when she heard the sound of breaking glass. She ran into the bathroom, looked up and saw my leg dangling from the ceiling. My calf was torn open, tangled in the broken glass, and I was bleeding onto the white porcelain surface of the bathtub. Elsie went back into the kitchen, returned with a chair and manoeuvred the shards of glass to free me. I managed to crawl along the roof and scale down the stinkpipe at the back of the house. Elsie bound my leg with a clean tea towel and embarrassed me by insisting I sit in an old pram she kept in the back shed for carting scrap wood. She wheeled me up the street to the hospital, along with her pet Jack Russell, Chico, who went everywhere with her. People passing on the street looked down at me in disgust, mistaking me for an overgrown baby. At the hospital, Nan embarrassed me further, arguing with the admitting nurse over bringing a dog into the hospital. She eventually apologised, took Chico outside, took her cardigan off, hid Chico under it in the pram and wheeled him back inside.

In the final weeks of my grandmother's life I sat in a wide window bay across from her bed. The ward was so new that the scent of fresh paint camouflaged the odours of illness. Three patients shared a room with Elsie, each of them elderly and seemingly unresponsive to life around them. From my window seat I could look down on the streets of Elsie's life and my childhood. The sun was shining and I rested my body against the glass to catch its warmth. I was a forty-year-old man at the time, with three children. As I glanced across to Elsie and saw the silent grimace of pain on her face, I felt myself shrink, helpless to relieve her suffering. Her body was connected to a machine emitting pulsating rhythms of life but, with the exception of mumbling the odd word and occasionally sighing deeply, Elsie herself did not make a sound. For reasons I didn't understand at the time – reasons that would cause me shame after her death – I couldn't bring myself to sit closer and touch Elsie. I remained at a safe distance, perched on the window seat with a paperback novel for distraction.

Jennifer set about organising the family, ensuring we each arrived at the hospital on time, in line with her roster. Only our mother refused to comply. She didn't mind having the rest of us under Jennifer's orders, but when it came to her relationship with her own mother, no-one was going to put her on a schedule. I'm now convinced that each time she left the hospital, Mum thought it would be the last time she'd see Nan. Not surprisingly, each bedside visit was savoured. She turned up when she felt the need to, which was each morning. Before Elsie had been admitted to hospital, she and my mother had spent each day together for most of their lives. As far as my mother was concerned, nothing would be changing.

She arrived on the ward early each morning to be certain she was by Elsie's bedside when breakfast arrived. The necessity made little sense to the rest of the family, as Elsie had stopped eating. My mother sat by the bed and chatted just as they had done around the kitchen table of a morning. A box of Dairy

Milk chocolates, Elsie's favourite, was left on the top of a narrow set of drawers beside the bed – *just in case she gets hungry*, my mother explained to the medical staff.

It surprised nobody in the family that Jennifer took charge during those final weeks. She was a career nurse who'd chosen the most challenging area to work in: acute care. She'd trained with severely disabled children, before moving into geriatric nursing and palliative care. One afternoon Jennifer and I sat and watched Elsie gasping anxiously. Although there was nothing I could do I panicked, worried that it might be her final breath. But then Elsie's mouth reached for air and she stabilised. Jennifer said that after working with terminally ill patients for many years she had learned that most people accepted the end of their own life with calmness, although a few went out kicking and fighting, which she also admired. It was the people who became petrified by a fear of death who upset her. She rolled up the sleeve of her shirt and showed me a deep bruise on her arm. It had been left there by a *mountain of a man* dying of pancreatic cancer, she said.

'He was in tears and wouldn't let go of me, begging me to do something. *Please, please do something.*'

'What did you say to him?' I asked.

'Once fear gets hold of people in that way there's not a lot you can say. To be honest, when it happens, we increase the medication. Morphine is the softener.'

After two weeks in hospital, Elsie was moved to an isolation room, an indication that death was close. Jennifer explained the reasoning with her usual dry and often morbid sense of humour.

'No-one likes to see dead people in a hospital,' she said with a laugh. 'It's the same reason the body is taken down to the mortuary in the goods lift, to keep the dead away from the front of house.'

'It's bad for business, I guess,' I quipped, attempting to relieve my own sense of dread.

'Oh, it is. *Living* people don't like talking about death, let alone being witness to it. Most come in for fifteen minutes, go home and watch reality TV. *24 Hours in Emergency*. They can watch other people suffer with a cup of tea and their feet up.'

Jennifer's career had hardened her more than I'd realised, although she didn't let it show, not when she was working with the terminally ill. Or when she was caring for our grandmother and managing the emotional turmoil of the family, ensuring with a combination of comfort and firmness that we didn't fall apart. And it wasn't true that people quickly visited the dying and vanished. In the weeks we sat with Elsie we became part of a community on the ward, each member doing all they could for those who'd soon be gone.

The morning after Elsie had moved to her single room, my mother arrived at the hospital carrying a plastic bag. I'd spent the night in a sleeping bag on the floor at the foot of Elsie's bed, listening to her rasping breaths between periods of sleep. I sat in a chair drinking a cup of tea and watched my mother remove a photograph from the plastic bag – a picture of my uncle Ruben, Elsie's youngest son. Mum sat the photograph on the cupboard next to the box of unopened chocolates. 'There you are,' she whispered to herself, her mother and her dead brother, a man who'd died alone, without family, in a telephone box in a country town with a needle in his arm. Mum took a handkerchief from her bag and lightly dusted the photo frame. I thought it was an odd idea to have a childhood photograph of Ruben in the room with Elsie. She hadn't been told about his death two years earlier. Once spoken, the tragic news would only have had to be repeated to her over and over again.

'If she wakes, Mum, and sees that picture of Ruben, it might trigger a memory in her,' I said. 'A bad memory.'

'And it would be a blessing, if she could remember him. He needs to be here with us now,' Mum replied. She adjusted Elsie's bedding. 'She looks a little better, don't you think?'

Elsie's painful expression hadn't changed.

'Maybe she does,' I answered in a lame voice. I was tired and had a sore back from sleeping on the floor. All I wanted to do was go home to my family. I kissed my mother on the cheek. 'I'll see you later.'

'Can you wait here for a few minutes? The florist downstairs was opening when I came in. I want to get her some flowers.'

'Flowers? Now?'

'Yes, now. We need something to brighten the room for her.'

I reluctantly sat by the bed, rested and closed my eyes.

Moments later, I heard the bedsheets rustling. Elsie moaned softly. And then she spoke. 'Water,' she gasped. I opened my eyes. Elsie was sitting up, barely. She lifted a withered arm towards a water jug sitting on the meal table at the foot of the bed, opened her mouth slightly and ran her tongue along her dried and cracked bottom lip. 'Water.'

I jumped up from the chair, picked up the jug and poured water into a plastic cup that had a screw-on lid and spout. Elsie watched me, with unfamiliar alertness, as I stood beside the bed and put the cup to her mouth. She drank greedily and water ran from the side of her mouth, down her chin. She smiled. A fringe of fine hair fell across her eyes. I gently reached across her body and tucked her hair behind her ear. She whispered words that sounded like *thank you*, although I couldn't be sure. She turned to her side and glanced at the photograph of her dead child. If she recognised Ruben at all, nothing registered on her face. She reached for the plastic cup and I placed it to her lips again. With shaking but deliberate effort, she lay her hand on the back of mine, rested her head on the pillow and closed her eyes.

Mum returned to the room carrying a bunch of flowers: gladioli. She opened a cupboard, found a vase for the flowers, half-filled it with water and began arranging the stems. 'You'll like these, Mummy. The flowers are not quite out. They will last longer for that. We'll put them over by the window.'

Elsie didn't appear to recognise Mum's voice at all.

Later that night I spoke to Jennifer on the phone and explained what had happened that morning. 'Maybe she's getting some strength back?' I suggested. 'It was only a few minutes, but she seemed a little better.'

Jennifer paused on the other end of the line. 'She's run out of strength, Michael.'

'How can you say that? She's a tough woman. You didn't see her.'

'She's always been tough. But from what I know, in my experience, what you saw, it's called *the knowing*.'

'The knowing?'

'Yes. When a patient rallies like that, it tends to come near the end of life. It's not about fighting or giving in. It's knowing that it's time.'

In my head, I recognised my older sister was right. It was my heart that didn't want to believe her. It also annoyed me that she could be so matter-of-fact, as if she were speaking about a patient and not our grandmother.

I woke around five o'clock the next morning. My wife, Alice, was curled in a ball on the other side of the bed. Our youngest daughter, four-year-old Melanie, was standing beside the bed, nursing her favourite bear in one hand and tugging at the doona with the other. Without a word being spoken between us, I lifted her onto the bed and wrapped her in my arms. Within minutes she was asleep, her breath warming the skin on the back of my hand.

I lay beside her, glancing up at the ceiling, at a sliver of morning light penetrating the room. I thought about the many nights I'd spent at my grandmother's house as a child. Although she'd never been an overly affectionate woman, as bedtime neared and we were sitting on the couch together watching the Sunday night movie on TV, she'd lean across and take my hand in hers. Her skin was always warm. And when she tucked me into bed a little while later she'd run a fingertip across my forehead, making the sign of the cross. At some point, she'd stopped attending church, but I found out years later that she'd never lost her faith in God and prayed of a night before going to bed. Knowing my grandmother well enough, I thought she'd probably decided to keep her options open.

Shortly after, when the telephone rang, I knew it could only be Jennifer. After the call I drove to the hospital through the empty streets. It had been raining heavily and the roadway was cleansed of dirt. My uncle Henry, Elsie's eldest child, now a man in his late sixties, was standing at the entrance to the hospital smoking a cigarette. His eyes were red and swollen.

'I was in there when she died,' he said, with a sense of pride. 'My old mum was not alone.'

'I'm sorry, Henry,' I said. 'Really sorry.'

Henry was a man from an earlier generation, not open to displays of affection. Regardless, he hugged me and shook my body lightly as he spoke. 'Oh, I'm sorry for you. You were one of her favourites. She loved cheek, Elsie. And you were the cheekiest of them all.'

'Is Mum here?' I asked.

'No. Your Jen has been calling her but she's not answering. It may be that she doesn't want to know the news. I'm waiting here for her. My little sister is going to need me, I think.'

I left Henry to his cigarette for company and caught the lift up to the ward. Jennifer was standing outside Elsie's room, speaking to a nurse. She kissed me, took me by the arm and eased me towards the closed door.

'You need to go in.'

I hesitated. 'I don't know.'

She ran a hand through my scraggy uncombed locks, as she

had done when we were kids running late for school with the nuns and I'd neglected to comb my hair.

'Go in,' she whispered. 'It will be good for you.'

I opened the door, went into the room and closed it behind me. My grandmother was laid out with her arms resting at her side. The grimace on her face was gone. She looked relaxed, peaceful and *young*. I looked from her face to the photograph of her son on the bedside table. I leaned forward and studied Ruben's face, noticing his own mass of curls and sweet smile for the first time. I'd never realised he'd been such a bold-eyed, beautiful child. I picked up a chair and moved it close to my grandmother, sat down and placed my hand in hers. Although her skin was cold, it remained comforting.

There was a knock at the door and Jennifer led our mother into the room. She stared with bewilderment at the body lying on the bed. 'No, please, no', she moaned, and then turned and ran from the room. Jennifer went after her. Our mother stopped at the lift and beat an open hand against the door before collapsing to the floor. Jennifer sat beside her and nursed Mum in her arms. I stood and watched them bundled together, puzzled that my mother, the woman who had cared for, fed and bathed Elsie for many years, appeared to now fear her.

Jennifer did not cry at all as she consoled our mother, nor later that morning, nor at Elsie's funeral the following week. It would not be until many months later that I came to understand that my sister had chosen to deny the presence of her own sadness and grief to ensure we were able to cope with our own.

THE LIBRARIAN

THE NEW SCHOOL YEAR. The girls returned from the summer holidays suntanned and singing Don McLean's 'American Pie'. Word for word. First day I was ordered to sit next to Spider Miller, in the front row, under surveillance. Spider lived in the same block of Commission flats, directly above us. Any time my sister, Nellie, complained about not having a father around the house, Mum reminded her to be careful what she wished for.

'Really, Nellie? You could end up with a father like him upstairs? Madman Miller. A dad is the last trouble we need.'

Spider should have been expelled at the end of the previous school year. He was only saved because he was yet to turn fifteen and the school was legally bound to keep him. Trouble first visited Spider last Melbourne Cup Day when, after losing a sizeable amount on the horses and enjoying the holiday tradition of getting blind drunk, his dad poured kerosene over the couch in their living room and set it alight. The fire would have spread and maybe killed the family except for the heroics of old Mr Ronson, who lived alone in the flat across the landing from the Millers. Spider's older sister, Geraldine, lying on the floor in front of the TV watching *Get Smart* jumped up screaming, 'Fire! Fire!' Her father sat across the room in an armchair, watching the rising flames, nodding his head in approval. Mr Ronson rushed into the flat carrying a woollen blanket. He managed to smother the flames, but burned his bushy eyebrows off.

Spider's response to his father's crime was to embark on a transgression of his own. He decided to burn the school down, and whispered his plan to me during the end-of-year school excursion to a big art gallery in the city. I was standing in the foyer staring absent-mindedly at water running down a glass wall when Spider sidled up to me and whispered in my ear, 'I'm going to break into the science lab, open all the Bunsen burners, wait for the room to fill with gas and light a match. Bang! The school will go up.'

I looked across at Miss Bow, honey-blonde hairdo, floral dress and red shoes. She looked like a *Bandstand* go-go dancer, and the girls in school loved her. Miss Bow seemed to love them back, but she had no time for boys, and had said that even at our best we were nothing more than a *distraction*.

'Bang, Spider?' I said. 'Blow the lab up and you'll take yourself with it.'

'I don't give a fuck,' he said.

I had no doubt he meant what he said. 'Spider, do you think I can have your Levi's jacket after you're gone? And your record collection?'

'If it fits, you can have the jacket. But not the albums. My sister's mad on The Rolling Stones. All my records will go to her.'

Miss Bow ordered us to join the group.

I pulled on the sleeve of Spider's school jumper. 'Have you told anyone else about this?'

'No-one.'

'Why are you telling me then?'

'Because when this is over and I'm gone, they'll interview my classmates. You can tell them why I did it. You know how to tell a good story. I'm handing my legacy to you.'

'And what will I say about why you did it? That it was your old man's fault?'

He lifted his head. 'That could be the reason. That's what my probation officer would likely say. But don't tell that story.'

'What do you want then?'

'Tell them I never got over Jim Morrison's death last year.'

'I didn't know you were a Jim Morrison fan. You have any Doors albums?'

'Not one. Not even a forty-five. But there's a headline in that. I could end up famous.'

Spider Miller didn't go through with his threat to blow up the science lab. The week after the gallery visit his father threw the family's TV over the balcony. It crashed to the ground three floors below and created an explosion of its own. He was arrested. The court certified him and he was locked away in a mental hospital. Spider did set a small grass fire in the paddock across the street from the school. He said end-of-year boredom drove him to it. It was after the grass fire that the headmaster tried to unsuccessfully expel him. And it was also the reason he found himself in the front row of the class, sitting next to me, on the first day of the new school year.

I'd been seated next to Spider, having committed a crime of my own on the last day of the school year, and also having my punishment held over. I'd enrolled in Home Economics at mid-year. Home Eco was dominated by girls and it was the place to be. While I was no chef I miraculously managed to bake a decent Christmas cake. In order to take it home and show it off to the family I had to pay two dollars for *my own cake*, an injustice in a supposedly free education system. Rather than pay for the cake I snuck into the cookery classroom at lunchtime on the last day of school and was caught red-handed with the Christmas cake tucked under my jumper by the Eco teacher, Mrs Arnold.

I looked across at Spider and smiled on that first day back. The arsonist and the cake thief.

A further punishment required me to attend lunch-hour detention, once a week, for term one. I was assigned to the school library to shelve books. The librarian, Miss Costa, dressed entirely in black and wore her silver hair in a tight bun. She also displayed a gold tooth when she smiled. I'd never met anyone like Miss Costa. On my first day of detention she explained that the numbering system on the spine of each book related to various subjects and categories. Although distracted by her glimmering tooth, I followed her instructions and shelved books for an hour while enviously listening to the shouts of kids running wild in the grounds outside the library window. Miss Costa sat at her desk eating a sandwich and reading a newspaper. She occasionally looked over the top of the newspaper, keeping an eye on me. Eventually, she called me over to her desk. 'When will you be eating your own lunch?' she asked.

'I'm not having lunch today,' I said, shrugging.

I saw no need to explain that I never ate lunch. I was usually too busy smoking cigarettes in the park, with Spider and the other smokers.

'You have to eat lunch,' she said.

I shrugged again and said nothing.

'You're being punished because you stole your own Christmas cake?' Her mouth curled slightly. I was sure that she'd smiled.

'Yes, I did,' I said.

'Why was that?' she asked.

'Because mine was the best cake,' I joked.

'And you couldn't afford to pay for it?'

The headmaster had asked me the same question, hoping to take pity on a poor kid off the Housing Commission estate. My mother couldn't afford the cake, it was true, but I didn't want anyone feeling sorry for me.

'Oh, I could afford it,' I lied. 'My mum gave me the money to collect it. I bought a packet of cigarettes and a milkshake instead.' I looked defiantly at Miss Costa. I expected she was disappointed in me but I couldn't be sure.

During the next detention, I noticed that she again watched me closely. Maybe she thought I was planning to steal a book. Before I left the library, she stopped me again and asked me if I enjoyed reading.

147

I'd always loved reading books. 'Sometimes,' I said, feigning disinterest.

She picked up a paperback from her desk and held it in one hand. 'Have you read this book?' she asked.

I looked down at a copy of *Tom Sawyer*. 'Yep. I've read it.'

She put *Tom Sawyer* down and picked up a second book. *The Adventures of Huckleberry Finn*. 'Well, you might enjoy this one.'

'I've read that as well.'

Miss Costa picked up a third book. *To Kill a Mockingbird*. 'And this one?'

I nodded my head. 'That one too.'

The school bell rang. I turned to leave the room.

'Please wait,' she said. 'Who was your favourite character?' She lifted the book a little higher. 'In this novel?'

Miss Costa was testing me. I guess she didn't believe I'd read any of the books she'd suggested. When I didn't answer the question, she prompted me. 'Would it be Jem or Scout?'

I could have said nothing, held my tongue and let her think the obvious, that I was not only a liar but stupid too. I couldn't help myself and set her straight. 'Neither of them.'

She looked surprised. 'Is it Atticus then?'

'Nah. It's not Atticus. He's too proper for me.'

'Who then?'

'Boo Radley.'

She leaned forward in her chair. She was curious. 'Boo Radley? Tell me why?'

'Well, he really says nothing much at all during the story. And you hardly see him, but he's always there. My pop, when he was alive, he told me that sometimes those who say the least know the most. And those who talk a lot, well, they talk too much and know little that matters. When I read the mockingbird book, I thought of my pop. Boo Radley was just like he said. He was the quiet one who knew more than others did – knew what was going on. If it wasn't for Boo Radley, Jem for sure, and maybe Scout, would have been killed by that drunken farmer.' I rolled back on the heels of my scuffed school shoes, feeling pleased with myself. I looked down at Miss Costa, searching her face for a frown or flushed cheeks.

She smiled to herself and put the book down on the desk. 'I've never thought of him that way,' she said. 'I suppose I've always felt too sorry for Boo to see him the way you do. You must read quite a lot?'

The hall cupboard in our flat was full of the books Pop left behind when he died – paperbacks and hardbacks. I'd read most of them. 'I do.'

'I looked up your library card,' she said. 'You've hardly borrowed a book since you started high school three years ago.'

She'd obviously been snooping on me. She picked up another book, a slim Penguin paperback. 'You might like this. It's a French translation.' She offered me the book. I looked down at it without taking it from her. 'The author won the Nobel Prize for Literature,' she added. I noticed that the polish on her fingernails was chipped. I took the book from her and left the library.

★

I didn't see out first term. Miss Bow did all she could to humiliate me and Spider except force us to wear dunce caps. The end came the day she performed a Jekyll and Hyde act in maths class. She ordered Spider to the headmaster's office for *whistling in class*. As soon as he'd left the room she picked up a guitar she kept by her desk, strummed a few notes and sang Joni Mitchell's 'Big Yellow Taxi' while smiling like a sunbeam. Spider bypassed the headmaster's office and left the schoolyard.

He knocked at our flat door later that night. We sat on the front step of the block sharing a cigarette.

'I'm not going back to school,' he said.

'What will you do?'

'My uncle is a union rep at the meatworks. He'll get me on the chain.'

'If you're not going back, neither am I.'

'You want me to see if I can get you work as well?'

Walking by the meatworks of a morning and hearing the cries of the pigs waiting to be slaughtered was enough to put me off wanting to head through the front gates for work. 'Nah. I don't know what I'll do, but it won't be the meatworks.'

Fearful of explaining to my mum that I wasn't going back to school, I put my uniform on each morning and left the flat with my bag slung over my shoulder. I'd meet Spider at the pool room opposite the tram stop and sit at a table drinking coke, smoking a cigarette and reading a book while Spider played pool for money. He talked a lot about the meatworks job without ever taking it on. Our lazy, enjoyable week ended when two policemen from the Gaming Squad walked into the shop one morning and accused the owner, Manny, of running a card game in the back room, which he did, most nights of the week. After interrogating poor Manny, one of the policemen grabbed hold of me.

'What are you doing in here this time of day?'

I looked down at the floor. 'Nothing.'

'Nothing, my arse,' he snarled. He turned to Spider. 'And you? Both of you should be in school.'

'I don't go to school,' Spider answered. 'I've got a job.'

'Some fucking job,' he said. 'Playing pool. Outside. Both of you.'

They marched us along a side lane next to the shop and told us to face a brick wall. The second policeman elbowed me in the kidneys and told me to spread my legs. We were both searched. Spider lost a packet of cigarettes, six dollars he'd won at a pool game and a flick-knife he kept in the side of a gym shoe.

Patting me down, the policeman felt something in my back pocket. 'What's this?' he asked.

I turned my head towards him. 'It looks like a book to me.'

He slapped me across the back of the head with the novel. 'Don't be a smart-arse.'

He read the title of the book, *The Outsider*, and showed it to his colleague, who was enjoying one of Spider's Marlboro Reds. 'These two are the fucking outsiders,' he chuckled. Must be an autobiography.'

We were put in the back of a police car, driven to the local station and locked in an empty room, where we were to wait until our parents were contacted. Spider would be in the clear, but I knew that my mum would be angry, being called up by the police at the factory where she worked testing spark plugs.

'I'm bored,' Spider said after an hour of staring at a police-force recruiting poster: *We Care*. 'Where's your book?'

'He took it off me. The copper who searched me.'

'What's it about?'

'It's about this fella who doesn't care about anything. His mum dies and he doesn't cry or anything. And then he kills another fella on the beach and he doesn't care about that either. Even when they catch him and lock him up.'

'Is that it? Is that all that happens?'

'Pretty much. Except I think what it's really about is that he really does care, but he doesn't want to believe that. He doesn't want to think too much either, because he'll work out he's bullshitting to himself.'

'That's the story of my life,' he said.

Spider paced the room, looking across at me the whole time. He eventually stopped and stood under a bare lightbulb hanging from the ceiling. 'Have you ever done that?' he asked. 'Bullshitted to yourself about something. Like you didn't care or you tried to believe something that wasn't true?'

I hesitated. Not because I didn't have an answer for Spider, but because I wasn't sure that I wanted to hear the words coming out of my own mouth. 'Yeah,' I said. 'I have.'

'Like what?'

'Like I say I hate school and I never want to be there.'

He looked shocked. 'And you really do want to be there? Fucking hell.'

'Well, not all the time. But some of it, the reading, talking about books and writing stories. I could be good at that if I tried.'

He craned his neck and stared at a crack in the ceiling.

'What about you, Spider. Do you bullshit to yourself?'

'Yeah,' he whispered. 'About my dad.'

'Tell me.'

'Well,' he said, not taking his eyes off the ceiling. 'I tell myself that I hate him and I want him dead. But I don't. He's a prick, for sure. But when I see him in the hospital, dribbling from his mouth and forgetting who we are, I want him to get better. I don't want him home with us. Not yet. But I do want him to get better.' Spider wiped tears from his eyes just as the door opened.

A copper stood in the doorway, looked at Spider and laughed. 'You can stop being a crybaby, son. Your mother's here.' He looked at me. 'Yours too, genius. And she's not happy.'

I never went back to school, mostly because I was given no choice by the headmaster. When he found out I'd been picked up by the police, I was expelled the next morning. My mother knew someone who knew someone else who got me a job in the basement cafeteria at Coles in the city. It was a lofty position, picking up dishes from the tables and taking out the rubbish. While my career prospects were limited, at least it wasn't the meatworks. The other workers at Coles were older than me. Many of them were migrants whose families had come from Europe after the war. During our meal breaks we sat in the sun on wooden fruit boxes in the laneway behind the department store, eating and smoking cigarettes. I was taught to swear in both Italian and Greek and fell in love with around a dozen older women, who teased me like I was a little brother.

When the days were colder, I preferred the storeroom behind the industrial kitchen, where I sat in an old chair and read the novels I bought in a second-hand bookstore in the basement of the Royal Arcade. I read two or three books a week and sometimes wondered if I'd wasted my time mucking up at school and ending up as a dishwasher. But the thought never lasted long. When I was a kid my grandmother told me more than once that regret was wasteful. 'You spend too much time there,' she said, 'you'll never give happiness a hope.' Coming from a woman who had experienced the deaths of two of her own children, and whose husband had taken his own life because he couldn't cope with grief, I took her advice seriously.

I was carrying a stack of dirty plates out of the cafe one lunchtime when I spotted the school librarian, Miss Costa, seated at one of the tables. I don't know why, but I tried to avoid her by ducking between tables.

She'd already spotted me and smiled widely, her gold tooth on full display. 'Daniel,' she called. 'How are you?'

I rested the plates on a vacant table and nervously wiped my hands on my apron. 'I'm good, Miss.'

'How long have you been working here?' she asked.

'Since … since I left.'

'Oh,' she said, and smiled again. Neither of us spoke.

The silence got the better of me and my cheeks reddened. 'It wasn't like the Christmas cake,' I said. 'I didn't steal it.'

She frowned. It was obvious she had no idea what I was talking about. 'Steal? What do you mean, Daniel?'

'The book you loaned me. *The Outsider*. I didn't steal it from you. A policeman, he stole it from me.'

'The police stole a book from you? How is that possible?'

I explained what had happened on the morning Spider and I were picked up by the police and how one of them had whacked me over the head with the book and then confiscated it.

When I'd finished the story, she laughed out loud. 'Oh, Mr Camus would have loved that. Are you still reading books? I hope so.'

'I read all the time,' I said, surprisingly proud of myself.

'You should consider applying for another school.'

Although the idea momentarily appealed to me, I didn't want to give the offer any serious thought and have to face *regret*. 'I couldn't do that,' I said. 'My boss here says I'm the best dishwasher he's ever had. He says I have a big future in the kitchen.' I laughed.

'Well, if you ever change your mind, let me know. I could write a reference for you. You were always a bit wild, Daniel.' She winked. 'But you were never dull.'

Miss Costa got up to leave. I picked up my pile of dirty dishes and stood, watching her walk between two rows of laminex tables. I didn't take my eyes off her until she reached the top of the stairs at the far end of the cafeteria and disappeared.

ANIMAL WELFARE

R UBY WAS A BELIEVER. In almost anything. We were sitting
in the front bar of The Guiding Star, a truckers' pub on
the highway on the western edge of the city. We'd marked an
old boy for captain. Handy for us, the publican rented rooms
off the car park behind the hotel. By the hour. Although Ruby
had done life hard, she remained a stunner who could hold
most any man in the palm of her hand, including me.

The three of us were sitting at a corner table by the
jukebox: Ruby, me and the old mark, a bearded grey-haired
driver wearing a baseball cap with a Hooters logo on the
front. He downed a shot of whisky, followed by a pot of beer,
while telling a story to the wide-eyed Ruby. I watched as she
looked into his bloodshot eyes. He licked his lips and studied
her deep cleavage.

'So, when Bubbles the chimpanzee passed away, it was
decided that they would do an autopsy. Michael Jackson, he was
paranoid about the circumstances of the death, convinced that

Bubbles had been poisoned, by one of the staff at Neverland, most likely. Michael was convinced that he'd be next.'

'Oh my God,' Ruby gasped. 'I saw that poor monkey on the cover of *New Idea*. He was so gorgeous. I can't believe that a person would poison a monkey. This world. What the fuck has it come to?'

'Bubbles wasn't a monkey, Rube,' I interrupted. 'Didn't you hear what this man said? He was a chimp.'

Ruby didn't like being checked in public. Not by anyone. 'Who do you think you are, Denny? David Attenborough? You couldn't pick the difference between an elephant and a fucking ant.'

I ignored the insult and passed the mark another shot of whisky. 'Carry on with the story, brother. We're listening.'

He lifted his glass. 'Cheers!'

Ruby and I did the same. 'Cheers!'

'So,' he went on, 'they took Bubbles to the morgue. It wasn't a vet morgue for animals. It was a private establishment where the Hollywood stars go if they've been interfered with. Examination is done on the hush.'

'Interfered with?' I asked. 'In what way?'

'I'm not entirely positive about this, but I think it's when they're heavy on the gear and play a bit too rough. A lot of that happens over there. The sex games they get up to. They're big on sex games.'

'What sort of games?' Ruby asked.

'Not sure about that either,' he replied. 'But I think they may involve kitchen utensils and small rodents.'

The handful of pills I'd swallowed earlier in the car park hit the spot just at that moment. I swayed from side to side on my chair and waltzed to the music inside my head. 'Go on with the story,' I said. 'Please excuse us for butting in.'

He downed his second whisky. 'They opened that chimpanzee up. With a scalpel. You wouldn't believe what they found inside him. I mean *deep* inside him.'

Ruby leaned forward, I sat back and we waited. And waited.

'What?' I finally asked. 'What did they find inside Bubbles.'

The mark's eyes twinkled with sheer joy. 'Inside that poor animal they discovered semen. Human semen.'

Ruby had just lifted a cocktail by the name of Morning Glory to her lips and spat the contents across the table in the mark's direction. 'That's disgusting.'

I couldn't believe that the truck driver could be implying that Michael Jackson, the same singer of one of my all-time favourite pop songs, 'I Want You Back', may have had sexual relations with a chimpanzee.

I downed my own whisky and jumped to my feet. 'Come on Ruby, we're out of here.'

She looked up at me then across at the mark. 'But Denny, we're having a good time.' She took the mark by the hand. 'Aren't we, having a great time here, enjoying a drink and a laugh?'

The mark ran a nicotine-stained finger along the back of Ruby's hand and winked. 'Oh yes, we are.'

'Well, the good times are over,' I fumed. 'You know nothing at all about Michael Jackson. You ever hear him sing "Ben", you white prick?'

'Denny!' Ruby shouted. 'Don't be rude to this lovely man. Please, Den.'

'You ever heard that song?' I demanded.

'Sorry. What song would that be?' the mark asked, laughing a little nervously.

'"Ben" – he sings like an angel on that song.' I slammed a fist onto the table. 'And here you go, insinuating that the same person, Michael Jackson, could have interfered with his own Bubbles. He loved that monkey. We're out of here.'

'Chimpanzee,' Ruby corrected me.

The mark grabbed hold of Ruby's wrists and tried dragging her across the table. 'You go where you like, chocolate. This honey is staying with me.'

Ruby let out a yelp. I picked up a chair and crashed it on the mark's head. He collapsed to the floor, his head opened up and blood covered his face.

The barman leaped across the counter, pushed me in the chest and looked down at the mark. Grabbing hold of a good portion of my T-shirt, he shook me. 'Do you know who this is?'

'Yeah,' I smiled. 'Mr Hooters.'

He shook me again. 'You're wrong,' he said.

'I don't care who he is. He's a liar. That's all I know.'

'Really?' the barman said. 'This is one of Benny Brooke's relatives. He drives for the company.'

As wired as I was at the time, the room suddenly stopped spinning and came to a crashing halt. Benny Brooke ran every illegal activity in the west, from drugs to trafficking baby formula. I'd bought and sold drugs for him in the past. His method of controlling his work crew was fear illustrated with colourful brutality. I looked down at the mark, his body writhing on the piss and alcohol stained carpet. Once he discovered that I'd split the head of his blood relative, Benny would make an example of me. Most likely in public and with a sense of theatrics.

'You'd better be on the move,' the barman recommended.

'I know,' I whispered.

'And I mean really get away. And don't come back.'

I grabbed Ruby by the arm. 'We have to go,' I said.

'Let me take a piss first.'

I dragged her out of the bar. 'We don't have time. Piss in the car.'

I drove out of the car park, onto the highway and tucked the car behind a road train. I blinked several times, trying to calm my vertigo and give myself some focus. The western sky was stained with the dark blood of the late afternoon.

Soon Ruby began to sweat and grind her teeth. She rifled through the glovebox in search of pills. She punched the dashboard. 'There's nothing here. You're such a greedy prick, Denny.'

'Take it easy,' I drawled. 'There's a joint under your seat. I rolled it this morning.'

Ruby reached under the seat and came up with a decent trumpet. 'Hey,' she said, 'this is some Havana. Wow.' She lit the joint and swallowed the smoke deep enough to hit her intestines. She passed it to me. 'I think you killed him.'

I admired the joint I'd rolled, stuck it between my lips and sucked on it like a starving baby at the breast. 'Nah. He was snaking around on the floor. He'll be fine.'

'Doesn't mean he can't be dead. And he's related to Benny. We're in some deep trouble, Denny.'

With that, Ruby started to giggle and was soon laughing uncontrollably.

'What are you laughing about?' I said. 'You just told me we're in the shit. I don't reckon that's too funny.'

She continued laughing and punched me in the arm.

'Hey!' I said. 'Enough.'

'Benny,' she said, giggling.

'So?'

'Benny and Denny. Yin and Yang. That's funny.'

'It won't be funny if he catches up to us. He won't stop at me, Ruby. Woman or no woman, there'll be pain for you, too. If he gets hold of us.'

She stopped laughing as quickly as she'd started, then turned and looked at me for a long time.

'What are you staring at?' I asked.

'You?'

'And?'

'I remember when I told my mum we were getting engaged. She was heartbroken. Do you know what she said to me? I've never told you this.'

I passed her the joint. 'What did she say?'

'She told me that I should never marry a dark fella. She said you're bad luck.'

'I'm no good?'

'I didn't say that, Denny. She said bad luck, not no good. There's a difference.'

'Doesn't sound any different to me. Hey, I couldn't care less,

Ruby. Next to your old girl that red-headed Hanson woman is Nelson Mandela.'

'Hanson?'

'Pauline Hanson.'

'Oh,' Ruby said knowingly. She took a final draw on the joint, unwound the side window and threw the remains out of the car. 'Yeah, I've heard of her. She's the one who had her dingo taken by a baby.'

'You mean a baby taken by a dingo.'

'Whatever. That's her.'

The road had gradually emptied. I looked out the front windscreen at the flat and empty west. 'That's not her,' I said. 'She's in politics. In the parliament somewhere. She's no good, that woman.'

'Doesn't mean a dingo can't have taken her baby. They don't discriminate. I've never liked dingoes.'

'I bet you've never met one,' I said.

She slapped me playfully on the cheek. 'Maybe not, Den. But I haven't met any serial killers either, not as far as I know. It doesn't mean I don't have a negative opinion of them.'

'You know the story about the dingo and the baby may not be true. Maybe none of this is true,' I said.

'What do you mean, *none of this.*'

'I mean nothing. Me and you. Nothing is true.'

'That's crazy. You should get yourself off the gear, I think you need a break.'

'It's not crazy at all. I read about it in a magazine. Some sort of scientists are working on this. Quantum people. Something like that. They say that none of this is true. We're in a giant computer game being played by a lunatic in outer space.'

'That's the most fucked-up story I've ever heard. You're the lunatic.'

'It doesn't have to be fucked up. If you're in the game, you wouldn't know any better. You'd only find out when it's all over.'

Ruby pointed outside the car. 'See that big tree up ahead? You're saying it's not real?'

'Maybe not.'

'This car?'

'Who knows?'

'That fucking cow lying there in the field, doing fuck-all? You wouldn't need a cow in the game. I bet the cow is real, even if we're not.'

Ruby was sometimes a difficult person to reason with. As it was, there was little point trying to talk sense to her when she was cooked, I was cooked, and when I'd possibly killed the relative of a criminal psychopath. I ignored her badgering and focused what little attention I possessed on the road ahead.

Pretty soon I could hear Ruby snoring. Loudly. I decided it was best to leave the main highway. I'd been out to the far west of the state when I was younger, working on the scam. There were small towns off the beaten track that few people had heard of let alone visited. I took an off-ramp, drove along a narrow road for another hour or so until I came to a crossroad. I pulled over to the side. Ruby was sleeping like a baby. A frightening sight.

I got out of the car and stood in the middle of the intersection. A sign to our left indicated that the highway I'd exited was eighty-five kilometres behind us. Ahead was a regional town, a good two-hour drive, and to the south, a local sewerage works. The fourth road, leading deeper west, was an unknown destination. I had no indication of what lay ahead except for the skull and horns of a ram crowning a splintered fence post. I got back into the car and set off west along the uneven road. The continual rocking of the car soon woke Ruby. She squinted and looked out through the windscreen. 'Where are we?'

'I don't know exactly.'

'Where are we going, then?'

'Where no-one can find us.'

The road became narrower the further we drove. Tree branches slapped and scratched at the car. I switched the headlights to high beam but could see nothing of the road ahead.

'Tell me where we're going, again?' Ruby said.

'I told you, I don't know. Sorry.'

'Don't be,' she said. 'You know this situation that we find ourselves in, Denny. It reminds me of that joke.'

I couldn't see that it was a time for joking. 'And what joke would that be?' I asked.

'You know?' she laughed. 'The where-the-fuck-are-we joke?'

Where I grew up, we weren't big on jokes. Life was serious for people with no money and no way out. 'What's that?'

'Jesus, you're dumb sometimes, Den. Where-the-fuck-are-we. The Fuckarewee tribe. You should know that. You've got some sort of tribe in you somewhere. You know, you're always going on about *my people*.'

165

'Get fucked,' I said, lazily.

'I love you too, honey.'

I slammed my foot on the brake. The road, now no wider than a track, stopped dead in front of a wire gate. I wound down the side window. 'Where do you think we are?'

'Like I told you. The Fuckarewee tribe. That's me. Queen fucking Fuckarewee.'

'I'm getting out to take a look around.'

The sky above was a clear midnight blue and the air smelled fresh, of eucalypt. I sat on the bonnet. The drugs had almost worn off. No matter, I felt a little high anyway.

Ruby staggered from the car. 'What are you doing out here, Denny?'

'Enjoying nature.'

'Christ. You've gone dog mad on me.'

She walked to the gate and stood on her tiptoes. 'Hey, Denny, I can see a light.'

'What sort of light?'

'A house light, I think. Looks like the outline of a roof. Let's go and take a look.'

We climbed a fence and walked downhill along a stone pathway. I could see a building up ahead, an old farmhouse with a light on a verandah that had collapsed at one corner. A vigorous vine covered the roof and the windows of the house, which was being strangled. We reached the verandah and stopped. I could see a light inside the house.

'Should we knock?' Ruby whispered.

'I don't know.'

The door suddenly opened.

Startled, I jumped back. A small and slim old woman stood on the verandah. She had the longest hair I'd ever seen, a silver mane reaching down her back to her thighs.

I heard a dog growl. A dark, wolf-like creature was at her side.

'What do you want here?' she asked, suspiciously.

'Well, we're lost,' I said. 'We – me and my wife, Ruby – we took a wrong turn. We stopped up there at the gate.'

'That's where you have to stop,' she said. 'There is no place else to go.'

'Right,' Ruby said. 'Right.'

'Are you two alone?' the woman asked.

'Yep. There's just the two of us,' I said.

'You best come in.'

I took one step forward and the dog showed its substantial mouthful of teeth and growled.

'Don't mind him,' she said. 'Manson is all bluff.'

'Manson?' Ruby wondered aloud. 'Is he named after the …'

'Don't worry. It's my little joke.'

Nothing, not the best cocktail of drugs even plutonium-grade coke could have prepared me for what we discovered inside the house. Cats lay along the back of a couch, on the kitchen table and above a bookcase on the far wall. Three dogs lay together in front of a glowing fire, two others sat under the kitchen table. A parrot, perched on a mantel, flew across the room and landed on the flue above the kitchen stove, which was covered in bird shit. What appeared to be a wombat was curled into a ball in an armchair.

'Fuck me,' Ruby said. 'A menagerie.'

'Oh, not really,' the woman said. 'Not in here, at least. The menagerie is out the back. I save animals.'

The scent of piss and shit was overwhelming, even for a man with occasional poor hygiene. 'Save them? What animals do you have here?' I asked.

'Well, your range of farm animals – pigs, sheep, cattle. Horses and chooks. And then I have the circus animals. The farm provides a refuge for them.'

'Refuge?'

'Yes. Humans can be so cruel to animals. I work with the young people. The activists. They rescue animals from the cruelty of the circuses and bring them to me for care.'

'You steal them?' Ruby asked.

'Don't be silly,' the woman snapped. 'I save them from torture and humiliation.'

I was genuinely intrigued by her claim. 'What circus animals do you have back there?'

'Currently I have a pair of miniature ponies, a donkey. And a monkey, of course. The circuses love to humiliate their monkeys.'

I immediately thought of Bubbles the chimpanzee. 'A monkey?'

'Can we take a look at it?' Ruby asked.

The woman smiled at the pair of us. 'Not now. Perhaps in the morning.'

In the morning?

She shuffled a few of the animals about, invited us to sit down and went into the kicthen.

'You don't have a drink, by any chance?' I asked.

'I have tea,' she said. 'Herbal tea.'

I rested my tired body next to Ruby's on the couch. Within minutes the cats returned and sat on us.

Ruby began sneezing. 'Get these cats the fuck off me, Denny. I'm allergic,' she said.

'Shut up!' I hissed. 'This old woman must live here on her own. There could be money in this for us. You shut up and be polite. We could make a killing here.'

'More likely you'll kill her. She looks near death to me.'

The woman returned with a teapot and two mugs. 'You two must be worn out,' she said. 'Drink this. It will soothe you.'

I raised my mug towards Ruby. 'Cheers!'

She winked at me slyly. 'Cheers!'

I woke in the early morning light with the taste of dust in my mouth, a pounding in my head and Ruby's breath warming my neck. I slowly managed to open my eyes. We were both naked and Ruby had her body entangled in mine. I sat up as best I could, which was difficult. We were in what appeared to be a shearing shed and, what's more, we were locked inside a cage. Ruby roused herself and sat up next to me.

'What's happening?' she asked, in a voice as fearful as I'd ever heard from Ruby. She was a tough woman, and I don't believe she'd ever considered that she might find herself in such a situation.

'Well,' I speculated. 'We are naked and we're locked up. I would suggest that the old woman put something powerful in that tea.'

'And then she put us in a cage?'

'I would say so. I can't imagine doing this voluntarily, of my own free will, no matter what drugs I was on.'

Ruby nodded her head in agreement. 'I think you may be right, Denny.'

We watched as a monkey entered the shed and hopped towards the cage. It rested one hand on the door, put an arm through the wire and opened its hand. Two peanuts sat in its palm.

'What do you think he wants?' Ruby asked.

I looked into the monkey's peaceful eyes. 'I think he's trying to be friendly. He has the upper hand here. We best not offend him.'

Ruby took a peanut from the monkey, shelled it, placed the nut in her mouth and bit into it. 'Hey, Denny, do you mind if I ask you a question?'

I took my own peanut from the monkey. 'Sure. What is it?'

'Do you think we're in that computer game you were telling me about?'

FLIGHT

THE CHILDREN'S MOTHER WORKED THE early shift at the supermarket, in the delicatessen. The job came with a uniform, holiday pay and whatever amount of shaved ham, cheese and olives she could escape with down the front of her maternity pants. She was out of the house by five, leaving Nish with his twelve-year-old sister, Miriam, who cared for her younger brother with a blend of tenderness and hell. Each school morning Miriam would drag Nish out of bed, make him breakfast of toast and jam, order him to scrub his face and hands, and stand in the bathroom doorway to ensure he brushed his teeth. Then they'd set off through the streets to school. Sometimes Miriam needed to pull Nish along by the hand, deaf to his protests.

Saturday mornings were different. Relieved of the school bell and the classroom, Nish would wake early, get out of bed, quickly dress and not bother with breakfast. He'd leave the house and spend his mornings wandering the streets and vacant pockets of land across the suburb. Since the back gate of his house opened onto a narrow laneway, he would firstly stop at a fence three houses down, put his hand through an opening in the timber pallets and pat the head of a yard dog starved of affection. At the end of the lane he'd cross a railway line and walk along a dirt track beside a fence topped with loops of barbed wire. The fence once separated scavengers and curious kids from the rubbish tip on the other side, but had gradually become riddled with gaps, allowing kids, stray dogs and local junkmen endless opportunities to explore and plunder the tip for its treasure.

A scrubby hilltop at the far edge of the tip looked across to the skyscrapers in the distance. While the city was close enough that the bustle of its crowded streets could occasionally be heard, it remained beyond the reach of children like Nish. The hill had been formed by decades of rubbish dumped from the back of tip trucks. It included termite-infested furniture, old machinery, the bodies of car wrecks and, if the rumours were true, the occasional dead body. Nish often stopped his walks on the hilltop, where he'd gather his breath and look across to the city and up at the morning sky before returning home.

Nish never forgot the morning he first saw the kite, lifting with the breeze in the sky above his head. The kite was brightly coloured and shaped like a butterfly. Nish craned his neck and stared up at it in wonder. It hung in the air for a moment before suddenly dipping, then swiftly soaring again into the soft blue sky. Nish followed its orange-coloured length of string towards the ground. An old man was piloting the kite, responding to the shifts in tension in the line that was attached to a wooden cross he held delicately in one hand. He wore a red hand-knitted jumper, baggy pinstripe trousers and a straw hat with the feather of a blackbird sticking out of the brim. To Nish, the old man looked like a circus clown. He moved closer to the man and watched the dancing kite, awestruck by the majesty of flight.

The old man turned to Nish and smiled. 'Would you like to have a go?' he asked.

Nish blushed and nervously shook his head. Although he wished for nothing more at that moment than to fly the kite, he didn't have the confidence to try.

'It might look difficult,' the old man said, reading Nish's thoughts, 'but it's not. It's all about *feel*. Feel the air. Feel the tension on the line. That comes to you a lot quicker than you might expect. My name's Arthur, by the way. What do they call you, young fella?'

'Nish.'

'Nish!' Arthur's eyes lit up. 'There you go. Nish, I had an older brother who went by the same name.'

Nish didn't believe it was possible. He'd never known of anyone with the same name as him.

Arthur continued talking as he slowly wound the nylon line around the cross, retrieving the kite. 'My brother, he fell from a boat one cold night in the middle of winter. I still don't know what he was thinking. Drinking beer and fishing should never mix. Particularly when you're out in the middle of the bay on a rough sea.'

The kite glided towards Arthur, who reached out, took hold of it with his free hand and placed it on the ground.

Nish looked down at the kite. Lying flat on the earth, it appeared more like a brightly coloured face than a butterfly.

'I haven't seen you here before,' Arthur said. 'But then I usually fly the kite of an afternoon. The wind suits me better. I heard on the radio that there was going to be a nice south-westerly this morning and I couldn't resist the opportunity. Are you new to the area?'

The old man's question to Nish made him feel uncomfortable. He wasn't used to being questioned by a stranger, even gently.

'You don't have to say a word,' Arthur continued, sensing Nish's unease. 'To be up-front with you, I've always talked too much. Have done my whole life. My old mum, when I was a kid, she used to call me Bird. Do you have any idea why that might be so?' Nish shook his head. 'Because I could never keep my beak shut. When I wasn't busy talking I wandered around the house with my mouth wide open, hoping someone would take pity on me and drop a scrap of food in it.'

Arthur picked up the kite, placed it under one arm and pointed in the direction of the city. 'I'm headed this way.' He doffed his straw hat to the boy. 'Maybe I'll see you again, young Nish.' He looked up at the sky. 'I reckon this wind direction is going to hold for a few days. I'll be by again, around the same time tomorrow. If you would like to learn to fly this kite, you meet me here.'

Nish watched Arthur shuffle down the hillside, kicking up dust in his wake. The kite flapped about like a broken wing on an old bird. Nish waited until the old man was out of sight, and slalomed down his own side of the hill, gathering speed as he ran. Towards the bottom of the hill he tripped on a length of rusted pipe and hit the ground with a thud, knocking the wind out of himself. He slowly raised his head and stared up at the empty sky, thinking about the old man and his kite, and wishing that he'd had the courage to say *yes*, that he would like to learn to fly the kite.

He heard voices in the distance, turned onto his stomach and saw a line of teenage boys marching along the railway track. He knew them from school. Older boys he did his best to avoid. The leader of the gang, Drew Cole, was swinging a golf club from side to side and seemed determined to wreak havoc.

Nish pushed his face into the dirt and lay still, fearful of being spotted by Drew and his posse. When the boys' voices gradually faded into the distance, he took a deep breath, got to his feet and ran for home. He sprinted as fast as he could until he arrived at his back gate and collapsed exhaustedly.

In the kitchen that evening Nish sat at the table and made himself a paper plane. He inspected the model and took it into the yard. His mother was standing under the clothesline with a mouthful of wooden clothes pegs and washing draped over one shoulder. Nish walked to the rear of the yard and climbed onto the rungs of a rickety wooden ladder resting against the fence. His mother watched on anxiously, her words of protest indecipherable on account of the pegs. Nish raised an arm and pointed the nose of the paper plane in the direction of the kitchen door. He drew his arm back and pitched the plane into the air. It dipped briefly before lifting, just as the kite had done earlier that day. He followed the flight path of the plane. It flew above the clothesline, across the neighbour's fence, glided between the overhanging branches of a gnarled peppercorn tree and continued climbing, above the iron roof of the neighbour's house. Eventually it disappeared from sight.

Nish's mother looked just as surprised as he was. She removed the pegs from her mouth and smiled at her son. 'Did you see that plane go?' she asked. 'That would have to be some sort of record.'

Nish nonchalantly hopped down from the ladder and walked towards the kitchen door. His mother stopped him, patted his mop of dark hair and affectionately pinched the tip of his chin. 'You might end up being a pilot one day.'

'Yes, I might.' Nish shrugged, as if there was nothing surprising about his mother's prediction.

Later, as his mother washed the dinner dishes, she told Miriam, 'Your brother is going to be an aviator.' It was Miriam's job to dry and Nish's to put the dishes and cutlery away.

Miriam looked at him and mockingly crossed her eyes. 'Really, Mum? I've always thought he would end up as a mad scientist, but I guess a pilot will have to do.'

'Don't tease your brother.'

'But he likes it,' Miriam added. 'Don't you, Nish?'

In bed that night, Nish thought first about the flight of the paper plane and then the kite he'd watched in the sky that morning. He decided he would take up the old man's offer and learn to pilot the kite.

Early the next morning, he dressed quickly, sprinted along the lane and didn't stop running until he'd reached the hill. There was no sign of the man or his kite. Nish felt disappointed. He rested his hands on his hips and looked towards the city. In the distance he spotted the old man, Arthur, walking along a narrow track towards him. Nish sat in the dirt and patiently waited. Arthur struggled to get a foothold on the hill and slipped back several times before he finally made it to the top. He took his straw hat off and gazed down at Nish with a vague look on his face.

Nish stood up. 'You came back. With your kite.'

Arthur dropped the kite to the ground. He pointed a shaking hand at the boy. 'And who are you?'

'Me? I'm Nish. From yesterday.'

Arthur scratched the side of his head and whispered the boy's name to himself, attempting to gather his lost thoughts. 'Nish?' he repeated until a memory switch flipped. His eyes lit up and he let out a gentle laugh. 'That's who you are then. Yes. Nish. Well, I reckon you'll have a bit more to say for yourself today.' He picked up the kite. 'But can you fly?' He winked. 'Let's get this beauty up there and find out what sort of pilot you are.'

Arthur handed the kite to Nish. 'Don't be letting go of her. Not yet.' He unwound the length of string from the wooden cross and slowly walked backwards along the ridge of the hilltop. He raised an arm in the air and cupped his hand, as if he was trying to catch the wind itself. 'Are you ready?' he shouted.

'I'm ready.'

'Well, hold the kite above your head and wait for my call.'

Nish held the kite aloft, both arms stretched above his head. The old man had the appearance of a worshipper offering a sacrifice to the sun.

'Go!' he called. 'Let her go!'

Nish released the kite. It immediately caught a gust of wind, turned onto its side and soared into the air, directly above them.

'Come over here to me,' Arthur called. 'You take hold of it.'

Nish took the cross from Arthur and held it in both hands.

Arthur placed one hand on Nish's shoulder and the other on the cross. He spoke softly to the boy. 'Here's the challenge. Soft hands we call them, soft hands. You're gripping the cross for all your life there. Have a look at them white knuckles of yours. That's not the way to do it. You need to *feel* the air to guide your kite. And to do that you need to work with light hands.'

Although Nish wasn't sure what Arthur meant, with the old man's patient teaching he managed to keep the kite in the air and gradually became aware of what Arthur was talking about as he repeated, 'Get the feel of her, the feel.'

When Arthur took his hand away from the wooden cross altogether Nish was sure he'd crash the precious kite. He began to feel anxious. He needn't have. The kite remained in the sky, responding to his guidance.

After several manoeuvres, Arthur returned one hand to the cross and together he and Nish brought the kite to the ground. Nish felt elated. While he watched Arthur wind the nylon string around the wooden cross, he noticed that a set of numbers, written in heavy pen, were written on the back of Arthur's hand.

The old man also looked down at his hand and then at his watch. 'I need to be on my way,' he said, appearing nervous. 'I'll see you same time tomorrow morning for another lesson?'

'I can't,' Nish replied. 'I have to go to school tomorrow.'

'What time's that?'

'The bell goes at nine o'clock.'

'That's no problem for adventurers like us.' Arthur tapped the face of his watch. 'I can be up here on the hill at seven-thirty on the dot. Thirty minutes for flying gives you plenty of time for school. You'll be here?'

Nish had no idea how he'd explain his new adventure, let alone his new friend, to Miriam. 'Yep. I'll be here,' he said.

'Seven-thirty,' the old man repeated firmly, as if trying to reassure himself of the time of their next meeting. 'Do you happen to have a pen on you?'

'No, I don't carry one,' Nish said.

'That's okay. I'll be sure to be here.' Arthur tipped the brim of his hat and headed back down his side of the hill.

'You're not going back there alone,' Miriam said, marching along the laneway behind her brother next morning. 'How can he be your friend when he's an old man? An old man can't be a friend to a boy. Unless he's your grandfather. And we don't have a grandfather. I'm telling Mum, and you are going to be in trouble.'

Nish looked over his shoulder at Miriam and began sprinting. She chased after him and soon ran her brother down. She wrapped her arms around him. 'It's better if we don't go. That way I won't have to tell Mum and you'll be saved a whacking.'

Nish was determined to fly the kite and wouldn't be stopped. He wrestled himself free. 'I promised Arthur that I'd meet him there.'

'Arthur?'

'That's his name. The kite man.'

Miriam blocked his path. 'You're not going back there.'

Nish started to cry. 'I want to go up there,' he pleaded. 'The kite was beautiful.'

'Stop sooking,' she said. 'You win then, we can go. But you're not to tell Mum.'

Arthur was at the hilltop when they arrived, the butterfly kite dipping and soaring across a patch of blue.

Nish looked skywards. 'See, Miriam? There it is, the kite. See how beautiful it is.' He ran up the hill.

Arthur watched him approach with the same puzzled expression on his face as the previous day, as if Nish was a total stranger.

'I've come to see the kite again,' Nish said, when he was close.

'Yes,' Arthur said, clearly a little uncertain about who his young friend was. 'Yes.'

Nish introduced his sister. 'This is Miriam. And she's come to see the kite fly.'

'Hello,' Arthur said, unsure if he'd met Miriam before.

Miriam watched the old man as he handed the kite to Nish. Although he didn't fly the kite with the precision of Arthur, Miriam was pleased that Nish managed to keep the kite in the sky. She'd never seen such a look of joy on her brother's face.

'Good boy, good boy,' Arthur said, patting Nish on the shoulder. 'Don't forget, soft hands.'

'See, Miriam, see?' Nish called to his sister. 'I can fly it.'

Arthur watched Nish closely, offering occasional instruction in a gentle voice. When the time came to bring the kite to the ground, the old man and the young boy worked together to ensure a safe landing. Miriam stared at the kite spread flat on the ground. She felt that it looked out of place. The kite belonged in the sky, where it was free.

Before heading off, Arthur invited Nish to return the next morning.

Miriam answered for her brother. 'He'll be here. We both will.'

They stood on the hilltop and watched Arthur stumble down the hill, slowly making his way along the track towards the city.

'He's real old, isn't he?' Nish said.

'Yep,' Miriam answered. 'He's real old.'

'Do you think he'd be a hundred years old?' he asked.

'Yep. Maybe more.'

The next morning, they returned early to the hill. Arthur and the kite had not arrived. Nish sat in the dirt and Miriam paced back and forth across the hilltop. 'Where do you think he is?' Nish finally asked. 'Maybe he slept in?'

Miriam kept her eyes on the track leading to the city. There was no sign of Arthur. Eventually, the time came for them to leave. 'Come on, Nish. If we don't go we'll be late for school.'

'I'm not leaving,' he said.

'We have to,' she said. 'I want to fly the kite too, but we've run out of time.'

'Can't we wait a little longer?' Nish pleaded.

'Okay, but only five minutes. If he's not here by then, we have to go.'

They waited another ten minutes and Arthur did not arrive. Miriam took Nish by the hand and helped him to his feet. 'It's time to go.'

Nish didn't protest. He walked beside Miriam, occasionally looking back over his shoulder in the hope he might see the old man and the kite.

At the school gate he gripped Miriam's hand. 'What do you think happened to him? Maybe he forgot us?'

'Why would he do that?' Miriam said. 'It was only yesterday.'

'Because he's old, I think he forgot to come. He forgot that we'd be there.'

They returned to the hilltop the next morning before school, and again Arthur was nowhere to be seen. Miriam kept her disappointment to herself. The following morning she ordered Nish straight to school without visiting the hilltop.

The next Saturday morning, he headed along the laneway alone, walking beside the rubbish-tip fence and crossing the railway line. As he approached the hilltop he saw a wing of the butterfly kite flapping in the breeze. He ran up the hill to meet Arthur, but the old man was nowhere to be seen. A rusted metal spike had been driven into the ground and the kite was secured to it. A cardboard label was attached to the pole. It read: *The kite is for you – enjoy its flight.*

Nish looked towards the city, puzzled as to where the old

man might be and why he'd left the kite behind. He untied the kite from the stake, laid it on the ground and slowly unwound the nylon string. Holding the line in one hand, he raced along the ridge of the hill and the kite lifted from the ground. Nish could feel the strength of the morning breeze in the tension of the line and he marvelled at the freedom of the kite.

Concentrating on piloting it through the air, Nish didn't hear Drew Cole and his gang climbing the hill. By the time he realised they were standing behind him, it was too late to escape. They'd surrounded him.

Drew pointed into the sky. 'What's that?'

'Nothing,' Nish muttered.

'Can't be nothing. I can see it with my own eyes.'

The kite tugged furiously at Nish, forcing him to lift his arm above his head.

Drew snapped his fingers. 'Give me the kite. I want to fly it for myself.'

Nish looked skywards. The kite defiantly ducked and weaved like a courageous boxer. 'I can't let you have the kite. It belongs to my friend, Arthur. You need his permission to fly it.'

'I don't care who it belongs to,' Drew said. 'Give it to me.'

His mates urged him on. 'Take it from him.'

'You can't have it,' Nish insisted. 'It is my job to take care of the kite until Arthur comes.'

Drew pushed Nish to the ground and ripped the kite from him. 'You don't need to take care of it. This is my kite now. Piss off, before I give you a hiding.'

★

Before Nish had even finished telling his sister the story about the stolen kite, Miriam told him not to move from the house and ran out along the laneway, her fists clenched. Crossing the railway line she spotted Drew's gang, standing under a large gum tree. One of the boys had another bunked on his shoulders, who was reaching up into the tree, trying to retrieve the kite stuck in its branches. The boy grabbed the tail of the kite and pulled it out. One of the wings was torn and the wooden frame was badly fractured.

Miriam sprinted towards the boys and crashed into the back of the one who was giving his mate a bunk. It was Drew Cole. He fell to the ground and the second boy landed on top of him, holding the broken kite.

Drew pushed the other boy away. 'Get the fuck off me.' He looked up at Miriam and laughed. 'What are you doing, you crazy bitch?'

Miriam picked up a splintered section of the wooden kite frame. 'What am I doing? You watch me, arsehole. I'll show you.'

She raised the stake above her head and drove it deep into Drew's thigh. He screamed out in pain. The other boys turned and ran. Miriam spat at Drew Cole. 'You ever touch my brother again, I'll stab you in the head.'

She collected the remains of the kite, walked home, opened the back door and called into the kitchen, 'Nish, come out here. I've got something to show you.'

Nish went out to the backyard and looked down at the remains of the kite lying on the ground. 'It's ruined,' he said.

'No, it's not. It can be fixed up.'

'And who is going to fix it?'

Miriam shrugged her shoulders. 'Maybe we can.'

Nish didn't look confident. 'I don't think anyone could fix it. This kite is all broken.'

Miriam rolled her eyes. 'Jesus, I went after it for you and brought it back. If you don't want it, I'll put it in the incinerator.' She began collecting the pieces.

'Don't do that,' he said. 'You're right. Maybe we can fix it. Are all the pieces here?'

'Not all of them. One piece of the wooden frame is missing.'

'Where did you find the kite?'

'Up in a tree. It was stuck. I climbed up and got it.'

Nish ran his open hand across the silk wing. 'Did you see them boys?'

Miriam concentrated on removing a wooden splinter from the palm of her hand. 'Nah, didn't see them.'

'You were lucky. They would have hurt you.'

Miriam clenched the exposed end of the splinter between her teeth. 'You reckon so, little brother?'

WITHOUT SIN

THE INCIDENT OCCURRED ON the day of Jonah Webb's fortieth birthday. He walked from the river camp to town as he did each weekday and Saturday morning, to Bobby Chuck's garage where he worked as a roustabout and general helper. Jonah mixed with few people in town beyond a nod of the head.

The day he was born, the white man who'd fathered Jonah took one look at the newborn and disowned both him and his teenage mother. 'That kid has something wrong with him,' he said, chasing any excuse to give up responsibility for Jonah. 'See the way his eyes are rolling around in his head. This kid isn't right. Must be retarded.'

The diagnosis of a fly-by-night farm labourer was enough for Jonah to be put into the care of his Aboriginal grandmother, who lived at a river encampment with twenty or thirty extended family, depending on the time of year. Jonah loved the river and enjoyed the freedom of bush learning, free of the shackles of a school classroom. Whether his lack of formal education was a genuine cause, or due to the prejudice of the town, Jonah was labelled *slow* at a young age and suffered the taunts of bullies as a teenager.

No-one knew for certain why Bobby Chuck took him on and paid him a white man's wage, cash in hand. A nasty rumour circulated around town that in exchange for providing Jonah work, Bobby would occasionally bed the boy's grandmother in the washroom behind the garage. The story was baseless and, although most knew it to be so, the truth was no substitute for the necessary denigration of a strong Aboriginal woman. The closest story to the facts was that Bobby Chuck's own father had treated the river mob harshly over the years, robbing them over the price of machine oil and kerosene while spouting words of such hatred that Bobby became disgusted with his old man.

Whatever the reason, Bobby and Jonah got along from day one on the job together. Twenty-five years later, almost to the day, when Jonah walked into the garage Bobby handed him a gift, wrapped in brown paper and tied with string.

'Happy birthday, Jonah. Forty years old. I'll have to retire soon and give you the keys to the shop.'

Jonah took the parcel and answered in a quiet voice, as he always did. 'Thank you, Bobby. That's kind of you.' He put the unopened parcel on the workbench.

'Hey,' Bobby said. 'Aren't you going to open it? You have to open your present, Jonah.'

'Not until I've done the tea.'

The day Jonah started work at the garage, Bobby had told

him that his first job of a morning would be to brew the tea. 'Put some steam in the boiler,' Bobby called it. Over the years, Bobby had told Jonah that the time had come to share the duties. 'You're no longer my apprentice,' he said. 'You're a man now.'

Jonah was a man. But he wouldn't have the tea ritual taken away from him so easily. 'Sorry, Bobby,' he'd explained on more than one occasion. 'This is my job, not yours.'

'Come on,' Bobby insisted. 'It's your birthday. At least let me make the tea this morning.'

Jonah briefly considered the offer before rejecting it. 'It's been my birthday plenty of times before this morning, Bobby, and I made the tea on those days. I'll do it again this morning, if you don't mind.'

'But you're forty years old today,' Bobby said. 'This birthday is a special one.'

'So is making the tea,' Jonah insisted.

Bobby let the matter rest. He sat at the workbench and waited for his morning cup of tea, wearing his lifelong uniform – an oil-stained boilersuit over one of Mrs Chuck's hand-knitted jumpers and a Castrol cap over his balding skull. He reached into his workbag, brought out a cake tin and placed it next to Jonah's birthday gift.

The two men sat in the early light enjoying their tea and apple cake until Jonah eventually opened his gift, a finely crafted hunting knife presented in a leather pouch. He held the blade to the light. 'This is beautiful, Bobby. Thank you so much.'

'This knife,' Bobby said, 'is the best you can get. You could skin a hundred rabbits a day, every day for the rest of your life, Jonah, and that blade will never go blunt on you.'

Jonah sat at the bench admiring the knife.

Bobby tidied up and then smacked his hands together. 'We best start work or it will be lunchtime and we'll have nothing to show for our day.'

Each Friday Bobby Chuck left the garage around noon to complete his weekly business. He visited the post office and then the bank before picking up the groceries for the weekend. He usually returned to the garage and worked for another hour or so before leaving Jonah to clean up and lock the garage around sunset, whatever the time of year.

Bobby was at the bank and Jonah was sitting behind the counter when a sedan trailing black smoke pulled into the garage and parked beside the bowser. Ray Jeans was behind the wheel and Kelvin, a cousin of his, rode shotgun. A third man was sprawled across the back seat, drunk and asleep.

Jonah wiped his hands on a cloth rag hanging from his overalls pocket and walked outside. Ray Jeans was trouble.

'You fellas after petrol?' Jonah asked.

'No,' Ray snarled. 'I'm looking for a bag of onions.'

'Oh, we don't sell onions here,' Jonah said, remaining polite. 'No shit?' Ray said.

Kelvin leaned forward and snarled at Jonah.

'No onions? We'll take some petrol then,' Ray said.

'How much?' Jonah asked.

'Fill the tank.'

Jonah stood at the bowser filling the car. Both Ray and Kelvin got out and stood by, watching him, making him feel nervous.

After the tank had been filled, Ray pointed to the dirty windscreen. 'Give that a clean for us. The back window as well.'

Jonah did as he was told, observing the young men closely all the while.

'This car's fucking filthy,' Ray said to Kelvin, lightly kicking a side panel. 'Hey, Jonah, give the car a good wash will you.'

'I'm sorry, but we don't have that service here,' Jonah replied.

'You don't have what? Can you try speaking proper?' Ray said, smiling at Kelvin.

Jonah was no fool. He knew that Ray was working up to trouble and didn't want to provoke him. 'We don't clean any cars here. Just the windscreen,' he explained. He held an open hand out. 'You need to pay me now. That's almost a full tank of petrol.'

'But I asked you to clean the car,' Ray said. 'I can't pay you for the petrol until you've cleaned the car. That's right, isn't it, Kel?'

Kelvin leaned against the bonnet. 'That's right. Fuck, Jonah, you've been working here long enough to know that. A full tank of petrol here comes with a free carwash. You stupid or something?'

Jonah looked over at Kelvin, who was grinning widely. 'That's not right. This is Bobby Chuck's business and we offer no free service.'

'You do today,' Ray said. He opened the driver's door. 'If you don't want to wash the car for us, that's fine. We'll take the free tank of gas instead.' Ray moved to get in the car.

Jonah held onto the open car door. 'You can't be doing this, stealing from Mr Chuck. He's a good man.'

Ray grabbed Jonah by the lapels of his boilersuit and dragged him away from the car. Kelvin wrestled Jonah from behind and pinned his arms.

'You listen to me,' Ray spat. 'Don't you be telling me what I can and can't do, you swamp boong.' He shook Jonah. 'If it wasn't for silly old Chuck playing the do-gooder, this town would get rid of you and the rest of them mongrels out at the river.'

'Leave him be!' Ray turned and saw Bobby Chuck holding a tyre lever in one hand. 'Leave Jonah alone,' he repeated.

Kelvin released his grip on Jonah, but Ray refused to do likewise. 'Fuck off, old man,' he said. 'I'll do what I like.'

'He says he won't pay,' Jonah said to Bobby. 'The petrol money.'

'Oh, he'll fucking pay, alright,' Bobby said. He took a step closer to Ray. 'You let go of him now and pay the money I'm owed.'

Jonah was a little shocked. He'd never heard Bobby swear in all the years he'd worked for him.

'What if I don't want to pay?' Ray smirked.

Bobby raised the tyre lever in the air. 'If you don't pay me, I'll bring this down on you and crush your skull with it.'

Ray looked to Kelvin for support, who was slowly backing away.

Bobby Chuck sensed the uncertainty in both young men and took advantage of their anxiety. 'Let Jonah go now, then pay me and piss off.'

Ray released his grip on Jonah, pulled his wallet from his pocket, took out a bank note, screwed it into a ball and threw it at Bobby. 'There you are. The money for the petrol with some change. Use it to buy yourself a sheriff's badge.' He and Kelvin got back into the car and roared away.

Bobby and Jonah worked quietly for the next hour or so. When it was time for Bobby to leave for the day, he cleaned his oil-stained hands in the washroom and stripped himself of his boilersuit. Underneath, he wore his second uniform of faded jeans and chequered flannel shirt. He said goodbye to Jonah, and was about to leave when he changed his mind.

'I'm really sorry for what happened today. That young Ray, he's a crazy one. The whole family are. But don't be worrying yourself over him, Jonah. He won't be back here tonight. Ray runs a card game Friday nights, in the old shearing shed on his family's property. He'll be kept busy with that. And I'm sorry for the language I used earlier. That's not me. None of it is. I just needed to put on some front, a bit of bluff. Just enough to be sure they doubted their own menace.'

Jonah waited until Bobby had turned away before he spoke. 'You shouldn't have done that, Bobby,' he said.

'Done what?'

'What you did before. With the tyre lever. Standing up to them.'

Bobby was puzzled. 'Why not, Jonah? He was going to lay into you. The two of them would have given you a hiding.'

'Oh,' Jonah said, actually smiling. 'You're right there. Two young whitefellas, getting a bit of sport out of me. Yep, they would have enjoyed that, for sure.'

'Well, why tell me to stay out of it? Would you rather me stand by and let them beat you?'

'That's right.'

'But why?' Bobby asked, frustrated.

Jonah created a fist and lightly punched his own chest as he spoke, raising his voice slightly. 'Because, Bobby, because,' he said rhythmically, 'because I am not some silly old boong. Today is my birthday and I am a man. And I have been a man for a long, long time. You're a good fella, Bobby, but this is for me to deal with, not you. Gotta stand up for myself to them boys.'

For the remainder of the afternoon Jonah tinkered around the garage and served the occasional customer. He knew each of them by name and they knew him, although few spoke to him other than to exchange small talk. Jonah didn't mind, he preferred his own company.

Just as he was about to close up for the day a driver pulled in for petrol. Jonah looked through the cracked windscreen as he filled the tank. The driver was Marlene Conlon. Her father had been the minister at the church Jonah attended as a boy, along with other members of the river mob. Marlene was a couple of years older than Jonah and he'd never spoken to her. Her father was a severe man who'd berated his parishioners each Sunday about the power of sin and the congregation's weakness in fighting it.

Back then, Jonah had been walking home to the camp one afternoon when he heard what he thought were the cries of an animal. He followed them along a narrow track into the bush. Had Jonah known what he was about to witness he'd have turned away, but it was too late. In a gap between a stand of trees he saw

Marlene Conlon on her back, almost naked, lying alongside a lay preacher from the church. She stared at Jonah until he turned and ran. He refused to go back to church and rarely saw Marlene again. When he did occasionally come across her around town, she didn't bother to look away or avoid him. She didn't need to. As far as she was concerned, he barely existed.

Jonah returned the petrol nozzle to the bowser. Marlene wound down the window and stared directly at Jonah just as she'd done years earlier. The secret they shared disgusted her and made Jonah feel uneasy. She handed Jonah the cash for the petrol. By the time he'd returned with her change, the car was gone.

He locked the garage, but forgetting his birthday gift he went back inside and retrieved the hunting knife and leather pouch. He didn't notice Ray and Kelvin until it was too late and they were through the front door.

'Hey,' Ray said, drawling. He was obviously drunk. 'That old prick, Bobby, has you on overtime. You know, I don't like him. The way he was threatening me today with that iron bar. I should have kicked his arse. You think so, Jonah?'

Jonah ignored the comment. 'What do you want here? I'm finished for the day.'

'We just come for some cigarettes,' Kelvin said. 'You have any?'

Jonah placed a packet of Viscount on the counter. 'There you are. You fellas need to leave. I have to lock up now.'

'We'll have two packets,' Kelvin ordered.

'No, we won't,' Ray said. 'Jonah, we'll take a carton. Thank you, brother.'

Jonah was certain Ray wouldn't pay for the cigarettes. Being drunk also meant that he was more dangerous than usual. He'd have to give them the cigarettes if he was to get rid of them. The cost of the carton would have to come out of his wages. As he reached across the counter, searching below for the cigarettes, the hunting knife spilled out of his jacket onto the floor and landed at Ray's feet.

'Hey, look at this baby.' Ray laughed. He took the knife out of the leather pouch. 'Oh, this is fucking beautiful. Kel, grab the cigarettes.'

'That's my knife,' Jonah said. 'You need to give it back to me.'

'Who says it's yours?' Ray said. 'I can't see your name on it.'

'It is mine,' Jonah insisted. 'Bobby gave that to me for my birthday. You need to give it back. Now.' As Jonah reached for the knife Ray thrust it towards him. The point of the blade stopped a breath from Jonah's throat. He froze.

'You want it, Jonah. You'll have to take it off me,' Ray said.

Kelvin raised his hands in the air. 'Hey, take it easy, Ray. Jonah here is just a harmless Abo. Leave him be. You're cool, aren't you, Jonah? There's no trouble here.'

Jonah stepped away from the blade. 'That's my knife. For my birthday.'

'Give it back to him, Ray,' Kelvin said. 'It's poor Jonah's big day.'

'Get fucked, the knife is mine.' He winked at Jonah. 'I tell you what.' He took money from his wallet. 'Shout yourself a flagon of wine for your birthday. On me. Grab the smokes, Kel.'

★

An hour later Ray Jeans was holding court in the old shearing shed over a solid drink and a card game, for money. He held the hunting knife in his hand and showed the other players how he had put it to Jonah's throat.

'You should have seen the look on the blackfella's face,' Ray said. 'He shit himself.'

The men were too busy rousing and drinking and slapping Ray on the back to hear the footsteps circling the wooden platform surrounding the shed.

Eventually Kel suspiciously sniffed the cold night air. 'What's that smell?' he said.

'There's no fucking smell except for you,' Ray said. 'You should have had a bath before you come out here.'

'Speak for yourself, Ray. You're on the nose yourself.'

Moe Grimes, who'd been asleep in the back of Ray's car earlier in the day, also smelled something in the air. 'It's petrol,' he said.

'Petrol?' Ray stumbled to the shed door and opened it. Jonah stood near the doorway with a lit kerosene lamp in one hand and a jerry can in the other. Between Jonah and Ray the wooden boards were soaked in petrol. 'What the fuck?' Ray said.

'My hunting knife,' Jonah said. 'I've come to get it back.'

'Well, you can't have it. Fuck off before I kick your arse. What's with the petrol, you mad cunt?'

Jonah waved the kero lamp over the soaking petrol.

Kelvin called out to Ray. 'Give him the fucking knife, Ray. The fumes on their own could blow us away.'

The men shouted and argued among themselves before Ray caved in. Quicker than would have been expected.

Kelvin threw the knife and pouch to Jonah. 'Now fuck off.'

But Jonah wasn't satisfied with the knife alone. 'Your clothes. Take all your clothes off and throw them over here.'

The men swore and cursed at Jonah but were persuaded to do as he instructed once he moved the lamp closer to the petrol spill. Jonah gathered the clothes and boots on the gravel driveway. He tipped the last splash of the petrol onto the clothes and threw the lamp onto the pyre. It exploded in flames.

'Hey,' a naked and freezing Ray called out to him. 'Don't you know that we'll be coming after you for doing this?'

'Oh, I know that. I know that real well, Ray,' Jonah said. 'But I have my knife. And I'm a man.'

LEMONADE

I'VE ALWAYS ENJOYED THE EARLY hour of morning, just before sunrise. When I was a teenager and had a newspaper round I looked forward to leaving the house for the darkness of the street. With the exception of the milkman and the early shiftworkers the streets would be quiet and I'd imagine I had not only the street, but also the world, to myself. In the back room of the paper shop I'd organise my round and leave by the rear gate, wheeling a rickety pram loaded with newspapers. The first light of the day would be waiting for me. On those mornings, I came to learn that each new sky – the shape of its clouds and its colours – was different, sometimes dramatically so, and other times with a barely detectable subtlety. Each sky was its own.

Many years later I was seated at the back of a crowded seminar room at the university where I'd taken an 'adult education' subject in Art History. Slouched on the lectern like a bored waiter ignoring his customers, the lecturer that morning announced: 'Nothing is original, of course. Originality is an outmoded concept.' In that moment I was reminded of my childhood and the hundreds of original skies I'd witnessed, each one produced in my honour, or so I'd convinced myself.

A little over a year ago now, when my younger brother, Billy, died suddenly, I started walking the silent early morning streets again. For weeks I was incapable of looking up. Instead, I followed my feet, shuffling aimlessly along footpaths or studying cracks in the pavement, searching for meaning in an effort to make sense of the incomprehensible situation I found myself in. I was grieving for my brother without knowing what grief really was. Many times, I slipped from the footpath into the gutter and sloshed through murky puddles. Or I forgot to stop and check for traffic at intersections, only to be abused by a passing driver about to mow me down. I must have walked for hundreds of hours in those months, losing sense of both thought and time. I'd eventually stop at the end of a long walk and search the unknown street corner I found myself on, wondering how I'd arrived there.

There were many aspects of my brother's death that made no sense to me. I felt angry that Billy had not told me that he'd had enough of life, despite the illogical nature of such a thought. I used to visit him once a week, out of duty as much as love, and did so under some duress. The visits were never enjoyable for either of us. He rarely spoke and was often agitated while I was in his flat, always eager for me to leave. On the day of my final visit to Billy's, I expected everything to be as it always was. But nothing was as it had been. And it would never be again.

Coincidentally, or so I considered it back then, some weeks before Billy's death I'd become preoccupied by a childhood memory of mine. It distressed me and I became racked with guilt each time it crept up on me. Each Wednesday afternoon as I walked to Billy's flat, I'd steel myself about the need to speak to him of the memory, to ask if he recalled it also. I felt a need to apologise, to explain that I was sorry for what I'd done when we were kids. But on reaching his flat and looking into his anxious face, I'd change my mind and say nothing. After his death I spoke about my guilt to our younger sister, Angie. When I finished telling her the story, she shrugged her shoulders dismissively in typical Angie style and said, 'Get over it. It's nothing.'

When we were kids it had been my job to care for Billy during the school holidays. Our mother worked day shift in a factory and it was left to me to get him out of bed, coax him to wash himself and eat breakfast. It was not a difficult job. Billy was shy, never answered back and usually did as I asked. He also enjoyed being around me. I didn't realise at the time – and not until many years later – that he looked up to me and was comforted by the assurance that I would always be there for him. We slept in the same room, went to the same Christian Brothers school and sat on the same couch of a night, watching American TV shows. It was only when I wanted to hang out with friends my own age, to wander far and wide away from the confines of the crowded public housing estate, that I didn't want Billy hanging around. But it wasn't easy to get away from him.

One summer morning, when the temperature was tipped to hit one hundred by the afternoon, and I knew that every kid who could escape would be heading to the nearby river for a smoke and a swim, I devised a plan to be rid of Billy. Before she left the house of a morning my mother's daily instructions always ended with the same strict order: 'Don't leave the estate.' Of a night, when she returned home, she'd drill Billy: 'Did your brother take you anywhere? Don't lie to me now.'

I was desperate to get to the river that day and knew I couldn't take Billy with me, as he wouldn't stand up to Mum's interrogation. So, I lied to him.

We'd finished lunch and were sitting on the steps below our flat. Most other kids had already left for the river and I was eager to get going.

'Are you thirsty, Billy?' I asked.

He was sitting close to me and had one hand resting on my knee. 'I am.'

'Well, I'm going to go to the milk bar and buy you a cold drink. I need you to wait here.'

'But I want to come with you,' he said. Billy always wanted to come with me.

'It's too hot. I need you to sit here while I run to the shop. I'll be quicker that way. What drink do you want? A coke?'

He took his time considering the options. Billy never made quick decisions. 'I want a lemonade drink,' he said. 'I love lemonade.'

I stood up. 'Good. I'll get us a bottle of lemonade each.'

He looked at me anxiously. 'But how long will you be?'

'Not long, Billy. I'll run and be straight back.'

All I'd intended to do was have a quick swim, a swing from the rope and maybe a cigarette. But when I got to the river there were more kids there than usual, and there were girls hanging around. Vincie Harris had rigged a speaker to a radio in the back of his father's beaten-up sedan, a car that fifteen-year-old Vince had borrowed for the day. I forgot about time and I forgot all about Billy.

It didn't register until I was racing home more than three hours later that Billy had most likely wandered off, in search of me. When I reached the estate I took a shortcut between two blocks of walk-ups. I saw my brother still sitting where I'd left him on the steps, his face flushed and sweating.

'Billy,' I said, surprised and relieved, 'you're here.'

'Where have you been?' he said, tears welling in his eyes.

I'd been so thoughtless about what I'd been doing that I hadn't bothered to manufacture an excuse to explain my absence. 'I … I … there was trouble around the pensioner's block. One of the old girls needed help.'

'What help?' he asked, doubtfully.

'Carrying boxes and stuff. I had to carry boxes up and down the stairs. That's what took so long.'

He wiped his cheeks. 'I'm thirsty. Do you have lemonade for us?'

I looked down at my empty hands. 'No, Billy. I forgot.'

I spent many days alone after Billy died. Often, I'd find myself at the end of Billy's street and would consider walking by his flat, knocking at his door and explaining to the new tenant that my younger brother had lived there for many years and he was now dead, that he'd died there. Instead, I'd turn around and walk back home, where I'd lie on the couch, exhausted, for some hours more.

One morning, as I closed my front gate, I immediately felt a stiff breeze cut through my thin jumper. In other circumstances I would have returned to the house and collected a jacket or raincoat. But I was no longer capable of common sense. Instead, I walked up the hill to the main street, looking up at the spire of the cathedral in the distance. The school we'd attended was next door to the cathedral. As I reached the top of the hill, I noticed that its oak doors were open. I hesitated before walking inside. The cathedral was empty. Cushions and Bibles were arranged along the pews on either side of the altar. I heard the echo of footsteps and saw an elderly woman, her back draped in a dark shawl, holding a cloth in one hand. Hunched forward, she was polishing the grain of a pew with the cloth. She glanced in my direction before returning to the arduous task.

I stared up at a statue of Jesus Christ, crucified. Blood streamed from his nailed hands and feet, from his forehead below the crown of thorns, and from the open wound in his side where he'd been speared. I'd studied the same statue many times as a child, as had Billy. It terrified me, as it must have scared my younger brother, although we never spoke about it.

The last time I'd been inside the church, more than a decade earlier, I'd looked up at the statue in disgust, believing that only a religion that wanted to put the literal fear of God into small children would decorate a statue with grotesque fake blood. But on that morning, months after Billy's death, my feelings towards the statue had shifted. The suffering endured by Christ, the violence evidenced on his body, now made sense to me. Punishment was real, and it did not easily forgive your body.

I heard the shuffle of feet, turned and saw the elderly woman standing behind me. She also looked up at Jesus Christ, made the sign of the cross, muttered a short prayer under her breath and moved on to another pew.

After leaving the cathedral I crossed the street and headed into the park I used to walk through each morning on the way to school. A gust of wind kicked fallen leaves into the air and it began to rain. Burying my hands in the pockets of my jeans I walked on and was quickly soaked through. When I passed the duck pond at the far corner of the park I heard a distressing sound and stopped to listen. Hearing the same desperate squawk a second time, I looked into the pond and saw a duck crazily beating a wing against the surface of the water. The other wing appeared to be pinned to its body. The bird was turning in tight circles and the noises it made became increasingly alarming, unlike any sound I'd heard before.

I ran to the other side of the pond and noticed that the duck's other wing and one foot were entangled in the same type of fishing wire we used to catch yabbies in the pond when we were kids. I felt angry. *You're a stupid bird*, I thought. It was the duck's own fault to have found itself in this dangerous situation. 'Get to the edge of the pond,' I called. 'The fucking edge.'

The duck continued circling and crying out in pain. With little thought about what I was doing, I jumped into the pond and waded towards the duck. The water was ice-cold and my boots sank into the muddy bottom. I reached the duck and tried grabbing a loose strand of fishing wire. The duck turned to face me and nipped my hand with its beak.

'Hey!' I said, a little more calmly than I might have expected. 'I'm here as your friend.'

I remembered seeing a duck protester on the TV news one night, saving a bird from shooters. He'd gone into the water, putting his own body between the hunters and the bird. When he reached the duck, he grabbed hold of it and hugged it protectively against his chest.

I looked this duck in the eye, dove at it and wrapped the bird in a bear hug. Wading back to the edge of the pond, I felt the bird nipping at my chest. I sat on the edge, tucked the duck into my side and gradually disentangled the mess of wire from its body. Once the duck's wing was free, it frantically flapped about, struggled against me and managed to free itself. I watched the bird glide across the top of the pond, skim the surface of the water with its webbed feet and finally settle.

'Excuse me, mate?' A park worker was looking down at me, his hands on his hips. 'What do you think you're doing?'

I pointed to the bird. 'I just saved a duck.'

'Which duck?'

'That one.' I pointed, and realised that there were many ducks in the pond and I was unable to locate my duck.

'Listen, mate. You can't swim in the pond. It's illegal. And you can't molest the ducks either. You'd better move on before I issue you with a fine.'

'I'd never molest a duck,' I said, feebly.

'I'm not convinced.' He smirked.

Any attempt to explain myself further was a waste of time. I headed across the park, my arms wrapped around my body in a futile attempt to protect myself against the cold. My teeth chattered and my body ached. I saw a bus parked by the main gate. It was the same bus that passed my own street, which was still a long walk from where I was standing.

The door was closed and the driver was in his seat reading the paper. I knocked on the glass door. The driver looked up, tapped on his wristwatch and returned to his newspaper. I knocked a second time. He reached forward and pressed a button on the dashboard. The door swung open and the driver smiled at me with a mix of amusement and mild disgust.

'You right?'

I wasn't right, of course, in so many ways. 'I need to catch this bus,' I said. 'I need to get home.'

'Well, I don't leave for another fifteen minutes. Sorry, mate.'

'It's really cold out here,' I said, shivering. 'Do you think I could sit on the bus and wait until you leave?' I asked, pathetically. 'Please?'

'Okay,' he huffed. 'Sit down the back though. You're wet through.'

'Thank you.' I got on the bus, searched for my wallet and couldn't find it. 'I don't think I have my travel pass. Or any money. My wallet, it's in the pond,' I said, before realising that offering such information was most likely a mistake.

'Of course, it's in the pond,' he said, nonchalantly. 'It's bloody freezing and you took a swim in the pond. Take a seat, my friend.'

The full weight of my body collapsed onto the seat. I

dropped my head and began to weep – for the injured duck, for my brother, and finally for myself. Resting my head in my hands, I sobbed quietly. I heard the hiss of the bus door opening again and looked up.

A woman walked down the centre aisle and sat opposite me. She seemed familiar, and at first I assumed I must have known her, but just as quickly realised I didn't recognise her at all. She had dark eyes and equally dark hair that fell across her face. Her cheeks were flushed and appeared to glow. She seemed as warm as I was cold and was wearing a thick woollen scarf. It was the most beautiful colour. Neither yellow nor orange, but both.

I'd cried in public before, sometimes while thinking about Billy. The woman could see that I was distressed. I should have turned away to avoid embarrassment, for both of us, but without understanding why, I didn't. I rested my head against the back of the seat and breathed slowly, in and out.

'Excuse me,' she said. 'Are you feeling alright?'

I looked across at her. Until that moment, I had never experienced a more comforting and open face. 'No,' I said, 'I'm not feeling alright at all. I fell, no, I mean I jumped in the pond in the park to rescue a duck. It was tangled in wire.'

As crazy as my story sounded, the woman nodded her head knowingly as if what I'd just said made perfect sense.

'And my brother,' I added.

'Your brother?'

'Yes. He died recently. He …' I began to cry again.

She stood up, removed the scarf from her neck and pointed to the seat beside mine. 'Do you mind?'

'No. No.'

She sat down next to me. 'You must be so cold,' she said, and offered me the scarf. 'You can warm your hands with this, if you like.' She wrapped my hands in the scarf. They warmed immediately.

The bus started moving but within a few blocks we were stuck in traffic.

'You must have been close, you and your brother?' she said.

'We were. But I let him down,' I said, my voice trailing off. I was uneasy about revisiting the childhood memory that had been dogging me.

'How did you let him down?' she asked gently.

'It's nothing,' I said. 'It's stupid really.'

She placed her hand on mine. 'I'm sure it's not.' She nodded towards the street ahead. 'It doesn't seem like we're going anywhere in a hurry. You can tell me. Only if you wish to, of course.'

I looked into the face of a total stranger and felt safe for the first time since my brother's death. She listened patiently as I spoke, about his deep attachment to me and how I had abandoned him one summer's day, so that I could selfishly enjoy a swim in the river.

When I finished telling my story, the woman moved closer and said, 'Your brother must have trusted you and loved you deeply.'

'How do you know that?' I asked.

'Well, I can't know for certain. But you left him alone for quite some time and when you came back, he was where you had told him to stay. He was waiting for you. No young boy would be able to do that unless he believed in you. Unless he loved you. I'm sure of that.'

'But I lied to him and left him alone.'

'And you returned to him. Never forget that.'

The traffic finally started moving again and the bus drove on. I felt numb, not with pain, but a sense of relief from a suffering I'd not been able to make sense of. I looked down at my hands, wrapped in the warmth of a stranger's scarf. When I lifted my eyes, the woman was standing at the door of the bus, her raven hair concealing her face. When the bus pulled into the kerb, she turned, smiling, and got off.

The bus was moving again before I realised I was still nursing her scarf. I jumped up and searched for her through the back window of the bus but could not see her. I got off at the next stop and walked along the footpath holding her woollen scarf in my hands. She was nowhere to be seen; it was as if she'd vanished. I wasn't sure what to do with the scarf but then I felt a stiff breeze. I wrapped it around my neck, turned and walked home, looking up at the clear sky.

RIDING TRAINS WITH
THELMA PLUM

Penrith Station was as broken as the shattered heart I carried. Those waiting for the train to Central had provided each other with more than the required distance. Some of us were sad, others miserable. One or two had to be both, judging by the look on their miserable *and* sad faces. The coronavirus had beaten us into a state of defeat, except for the chosen few who were tagged 'essential workers' by the government. It was our job to drip-feed an economy twice fucked, first by iso, then by the elusive *market*. Initially, I'd enjoyed the luxury of unemployment. I was Mr Job-Seeker-Keeper, lounging at home for three beautiful months in my flannelette pyjamas and house socks, choreographing my TikTok to the Phil Collins hit 'Against All Odds'. And then, unfortunately, Centrelink found me a job in a hospital kitchen.

There was pain on the faces of my fellow commuters, who, like me, had savoured the endless weeks of sleeping in and baked beans on toast for *brunch*, a luxury previously granted only to those above us on the socioeconomic pecking order. As workers such as myself served no intellectual or cultural purpose, we'd avoided the Zooming and Webexing routine of the intelligentsia and had been left to mainline on day-and-night-time commercial TV. When I was a kid and hated school I would get down on my knees in the bedroom and pray that every day might become Sunday. God was finally on my side thirty years later.

I leaned forward and searched the length of the platform. We were a pitiful gathering. Except for the teenage girl in black boots, black jeans and a black hoodie with the black, red and yellow Aboriginal flag emblazoned on the back. She had fierce brown eyes, wore a set of gold headphones and danced in silence; no sound, except for the sharp beat of the heel of a boot slapping concrete and the occasional shout of 'Hey!', her fist raised in the air.

When the train arrived we dutifully shuffled into the carriages. An announcement reminded us to sit the required distance apart. I took a seat by the window, opposite a decidedly artistic-looking couple dressed similarly in woollen layers over black. Each of them scribbled away in a Moleskine notebook. They looked an earnest pair. I wondered if they were professional mourners. Or perhaps poets, down from the Blue Mountains for the day, a trip into the metropolis in search of material. I eyed them with suspicion, wondering how the literati had escaped lockdown.

Our carriage had been pasted with rail network signs ordering us to *spread*, wash our hands regularly, cough in the crook of an arm, preferably one's own I assumed, and consider face masks, advice the passenger sitting across the aisle from me should have heeded. The snarl on his face was so frozen I wondered if he'd had a stroke. He was staring at our girl in black, sitting opposite him, who continued to tap the heel of her boot and occasionally shout, 'Hey! Hey!' She obviously had the one song on repeat.

He was wearing a T-shirt with the words *Pussies Lives Matter* emblazoned across the chest. Below the slogan was a colour photograph of Queen Elizabeth, the second one. The odd combination of words and image made no sense to me, although I admit I'm no expert on the power of subliminal marketing. If, as someone once wrote, *the revolution is just a T-shirt away*, we were in trouble. Both he and his peculiar call to arms seemed out of place on a train carriage that otherwise resembled a United Nations touring party. I sensed his intention was to veto our collective goodwill.

I'd read a week earlier that the number of languages spoken in Sydney exceeded two hundred and fifty, and despite our social distancing I could hear many of them ranging through the carriage. Only myself, the poets and *PLM* remained silent. The couple seemed to have bedded themselves in the private universe of metaphor, continuing to scratch away on their acid-free paper, occasionally looking over the top of their designer glasses. But not him. *PLM* leaned forward, dialled the snarl up several notches and looked into the eyes of the girl in black. If she was intimidated, it didn't show. She looked back at him, managed a smile and continued with the heel tapping, introducing a slight hip sway into her routine.

I don't like conflict. I grew up in a crazy house with an even crazier father, who was always angry. His party trick was breaking cheap furniture in half, including the three-seater couch we'd bought on a forty-eight month interest-free contract. Within weeks of purchasing it we had already fallen behind on our payments. A debt collector came to the house one time demanding an on-the-spot payment or a return of the maroon crushed-velvet Jason recliner. My old man took the tattooed, head-shaven thug through the house into the backyard and pointed at Rogue, our brindle pig dog, who was lounging in the remains of the armchair, most of which he'd chewed at and eaten. 'There it is,' the old man said. 'It was never comfortable.'

When my mother left us, out of the blue, he set fire to the house and stood on the nature strip with me and my younger brother. We watched the house burn to the ground before he called 000. I was always nervous around him. Thankfully, he's been dead for a long time. Heart attack. Some men, particularly angry men like my father and Mr Pussies Lives across the aisle, appear to forever be on the verge of exploding. Occasionally they do so, and leave mayhem in their wake.

The train pulled into Parramatta Station and the girl in black stood up. I expected she was about to get off the train, but she didn't. She stretched her body and turned around, ensuring that both her back and the Aboriginal flag were more or less in *PLM*'s face. His snarl shifted to a look of disgust, underlined with rage. He glanced over at me, and then to the other commuters, to gauge our reaction. There was none. The girl began to toe-tap along the aisle like an old-school tap dancer, hey-heying some more.

A few travellers turned away and concentrated on the flat expanse of the endless west outside the window. Others followed the girl's movements, enjoying the performance. A pair of slightly-built young fellas, resembling apprentice jockeys, began clapping hands in time to her dance. Even the poets detected something of value. At that moment, I saw my dad's mad eyes in the face of the man opposite, who had managed to link the head of the British monarchy, felines, Black Lives Matter and a passionate hatred for a song he couldn't hear. I feared for the girl's life.

She carried no such anxiety. She returned to her seat and spread her legs as widely as he'd done. She sat forward and looked into his eyes. The face-off lasted barely thirty seconds, before *PLM* blinked and turned away.

The conductor announced we were about to arrive at Redfern Station. The girl in black stood, pointed a finger at *PLM*, pronounced a final 'Hey!' followed with a delightful 'Fuck that!' and left the train.

He looked over at me, no doubt seeking an ally. 'They think they own the country. Do you know that?'

One of the poets, the woman, leaned across the aisle and offered him literary advice. 'Or you could say the country owns them. The statement has greater resonance, I feel.'

She smiled at me and I smiled back. Pussy Lives Matter slumped in his seat, a broken man.

ACKNOWLEDGEMENTS

I MUST THANK EVERYONE AT the University of Queensland Press for supporting my writing over the past decade. It is important for me, knowing that people value what I am trying to achieve with my work.

Three stories in this collection, 'After Life', 'Bicycle Thieves' and 'Lemonade' are dedicated to the life of my little brother, Wayne, who died in 2019. I initially hesitated to write about Wayne, but changed my mind, accepting that I want people to realise what a wonder he was – and is.

I want to thank Jenna Lee, who designed this book. Jenna is an artist able to see the life of words. I am fortunate to have worked with her.

The title of both the opening story and the collection is from a poem, 'dark as last night', by Anne-Marie Te Whiu. I was struck by the depth of four words that provided inspiration for the mood of my work. As the collection developed, so did the need to retain and recognise these words. The poem, published with Red Room Poetry, can be read at redroomcompany.org.

The death of my brother devastated our family, but we held tight, anchored by the courage of my mother, Dawn, the ongoing support of my stepfather, Phillip, and an ever-growing mob. So, please allow me to thank my partner Sara, Erin and Dan, Siobhan and Nick, Drew, Grace, Nina, Brian, Debbie, Tracey and Phil, and a cast of spouses, nephews, nieces, cousins, and aunties and uncles.

The best time in the life for this author has come with being a grandfather – 'Pa'. Isabel, beginning school in 2021, is already a rock of courage. I love you, Bel, for your stubbornness and energy – keep it up! Archie has inherited Wayne's birth trait of gentleness. Thank God. We don't need hard men in our family, but we do need your loving soul, Archie. And finally, born on 27 November 2020, in London (of all places!), my third grandchild, Charlie Burke. We will see you at home soon, Charlie, as we need to explore the laneways of our lives.

The author would also like to acknowledge the following publications where versions of these stories have appeared:

- 'Bobby Moses' in *Griffith Review 63: Writing the Country*, Griffith Review, Brisbane, 2019.
- 'The Blood Bank: A Love Story' in *The Saturday Paper*, 25 April 2020.
- 'The Manger' in *Choice Words: A Collection of Writing about Abortion*, edited by Louise Swinn, Allen & Unwin, Sydney, 2019.

ACKNOWLEDGEMENTS

- 'Together' in *The Saturday Paper*, 21 December 2019.
- 'The Librarian' in *The Big Issue*, August 2018.
- 'Flight' in *New Australian Fiction 2019*, Kill Your Darlings, Melbourne, 2019.
- 'Riding Trains with Thelma Plum' in *The Saturday Paper*, 1 August 2020.

THE WHITE GIRL
Tony Birch

'Odette, be sensible. Sissy cannot leave this town.' Shea threw his hands in the air. 'Listen to me, please, Odette. It's not as if your Sissy is a white girl.'

Odette Brown has lived her whole life on the fringes of a small country town. Raising her granddaughter Sissy on her own, Odette has managed to stay under the radar of the welfare authorities who are removing Aboriginal children from their communities. When the menacing Sergeant Lowe arrives in town, determined to fully enforce the law, any freedom that Odette and Sissy enjoy comes under grave threat. Odette must make an impossible choice to protect her family.

In *The White Girl*, Tony Birch has created memorable characters whose capacity for love and courage are a timely reminder of the endurance of the human spirit.

'... it is a rare thing for a novel to tell a gripping story while also engaging more broadly with the continuing dispossession and violence that are our uneasy inheritance.' *The Saturday Paper*

'Tony Birch's new novel goes to the heart of black and white relations in Australia, and puts the voices of women front and centre.' *The Big Issue*

'Rich in humanity and purpose, and hope. *The White Girl* is worth your time and will reward you over and over again.' *Australian Book Review*

ISBN 978 0 7022 6305 7

UQP

GHOST RIVER
Tony Birch

Stories of the river were told across the city. There wasn't a child living within reach of the water who hadn't grown up warned away from it with tales of dead trees lurking in the darkness of the muddy riverbed, ready to snatch the leg of a boy or girl braving its filthy water.

The river is a place of history and secrets. For Ren and Sonny, two unlikely friends, it's a place of freedom and adventure. For a group of storytelling vagrants, it's a refuge. And for the isolated daughter of a cult reverend, it's an escape.

Each time they visit, another secret slips into its ancient waters. But change and trouble are coming – to the river and to the lives of those who love it. Who will have the courage to fight and what will be the cost?

'The hard language always underpinned by a battler's romanticism, a belief in people, the world, the spirit, and the struggle.' *The Saturday Age*

'Birch is a natural storyteller ... A vivid portrait of his central characters ... in *Ghost River* we find a welcome and vital addition to his body of work.' *Australian Book Review*

'This is a beautiful novel, part coming of age story, part history of inner Melbourne.' *Readings*

ISBN 978 0 7022 6339 2

COMMON PEOPLE
Tony Birch

In this unforgettable collection, Tony Birch introduces a cast of characters from all walks of life. These remarkable and surprising stories capture common people caught up in the everyday business of living and the struggle to survive. From two single mothers on the most unlikely night shift to a homeless man unexpectedly faced with the miracle of a new life, Birch's stories are set in gritty urban refuges and battling regional communities. His deftly drawn characters find unexpected signs of hope in a world where beauty can be found on every street corner – a message on a T-shirt, a friend in a stray dog or a star in the night sky.

Common People shines a light on human nature and how the ordinary kindness of strangers can have extraordinary results. With characteristic insight and restraint, Tony Birch reinforces his reputation as a master storyteller.

'The stories are varied, sustained and filled with beautiful writing that shows a rare talent for getting inside the minds of a huge cast of characters. There is not one word out of place.' *The Herald Sun*

'Birch throws us straight into the action. There is always urgency and vitality in his stories; there is always a wide terrain. Characters are immediately and completely drawn with just a few words, and do not fit into easily defined moulds.' *Weekend Australian*

ISBN 978 0 7022 6582 2